RUN!
Warriors Series, Book 12

By

Ty Patterson

RUN! is a work of fiction. Names, characters, businesses, places, events, and incidents are either the products of the author's imagination or used in a fictitious manner. Any resemblance to actual persons, living or dead, or actual events is purely coincidental. All rights reserved. This book or any portion thereof may not be reproduced, or used in any manner whatsoever without the express written permission of the publisher except for the use of brief quotations in a book review.

Copyright © 2017 by Ty Patterson
All rights reserved
Published by Three Aces Publishing
Visit the author site: http://www.typatterson.com

License notes:
This ebook is licensed for your personal enjoyment only. This ebook may not be re-sold or given away to other people. If you would like to share this book with another person, please purchase an additional copy for each person you share it with. If you're reading this book and did not purchase it, or it was not purchased for you only, then please return it and purchase your own copy. If the author gave you an advance reader or a beta reader copy, please do not share it with any other person. Thank you for respecting the hard work of this author.

Publisher's Note:
The publisher and author do not have any control over and do not assume any responsibility for author or third-party websites or their content.

No part of this book may be reproduced, scanned, or distributed in any printed or electronic form without express written permission from the publisher. The scanning, uploading, and distribution of this book via the Internet or any other means without permission of the publisher is illegal and punishable by law. Please do not participate in or encourage piracy of copyrighted materials in violation of the author's rights. Purchase only authorized editions.

Original Cover Design: Nathan Wampler
Interior Formatting: Tugboat Design

Books by Ty Patterson

Warriors Series Shorts
This is a series of novellas that link to the Warriors Series thrillers

Zulu Hour, Warriors Series Shorts, Book 1 (set before *The Warrior*)
The Watcher, Warriors Series Shorts, Book 2 (set between *The Warrior* and *The Warrior Code*)
The Shadow, Warriors Series Shorts, Book 3 (set before *The Warrior*)
The Man From Congo, Warriors Series Shorts, Book 4
Warriors Series Shorts, Boxset I, Books 1-4
The Texan, Warriors Series Shorts, Book 5
The Heavies, Warriors Series Shorts, Book 6
The Cab Driver, Warriors Series Shorts, Book 7

Gemini Series

Dividing Zero, Gemini Series, Book 1
Defending Cain, Gemini Series, Book 2
I Am Missing, Gemini Series, Book 3

Warriors Series

The Warrior, Warriors series, Book 1
The Reluctant Warrior, Warriors series, Book 2
The Warrior Code, Warriors series, Book 3
The Warrior's Debt, Warriors series, Book 4
Flay, Warriors series, Book 5
Behind You, Warriors series, Book 6
Hunting You, Warriors series, Book 7
Zero, Warriors series, Book 8
Death Club, Warriors series, Book 9
Trigger Break, Warriors series, Book 10
Scorched Earth, Warriors series, Book 11
RUN!, Warriors series, Book 12
Warriors series Boxset, Books 1-4
Warriors series Boxset II, Books 5-8
Warriors series Boxset III, Books 1-8

Sign up to Ty Patterson's mailing list, and get The Warrior, #1 in the USA Today Bestselling Warriors Series, free. Be the first to know about new releases and deals.

Check out Ty on Amazon, on iTunes, on Kobo, on Google Play, and on Barnes and Noble.

Acknowledgments

No book is a single person's product. I am privileged that *RUN!* has benefited from the input of several great people.

Molly Birch, David T. Blake, Tracy Boulet, Patricia Burke, Mark Campbell, Tricia Cullerton, Claire Forgacs, Dave Davis, Sylvia Foster, Cary Lory Becker, Charlie Carrick, Pat Ellis, Dori Barrett, Simon Alphonso, Dave Davis, V. Elizabeth Perry, Ann Finn, Pete Bennett, Eric Blackburn, Margaret Harvey, David Hay, Jim Lambert, Suzanne Jackson Mickelson, Tricia Terry Pellman, Jimmy Smith, Theresa, and Brad Werths, who are my beta readers and who helped shape my book, my launch team for supporting me, Doreen Martens for her editing, and Donna Rich for her proofreading.

Dedications

To Michelle Rose Dunn, Debbie Bruns Gallant, Tom Gallant, and Cheri Gerhardt, for supporting me.

To all the men and women in uniform who make it possible for us to enjoy our freedom.

Truth will ultimately prevail where there is pains to bring it to light.
—George Washington

Catch!

Part I

Chapter 1

He came from Beirut. He came from war. His name was Waleed Omar Bilal, but not many remembered that name. Namir was what everyone called him—those who feared him, and there were many of them, and those who respected him as well.

Namir. Leopard.

They had started calling him that because of his ability to strike without warning and disappear into nothingness.

No one knew when he would come, or from where. All knew that when he left, there would be death and destruction in his wake.

The name had originated in a small village in the Bekaa Valley of Lebanon.

He and his small band of men had ambushed and captured an American convoy of thirty. He had killed most of the men and, after torturing the survivors, had left them to die in the heat.

Namir. That's when his men had started calling him by that name.

Namir had known war all his life. He was born during a Lebanese army bombing raid in the valley.

He had seen his parents murdered by Maronite Christian guerillas.

That horrific incident stayed with him. He grew up being reared by neighbors and militants.

The earliest memory he had was of his parents dying.

The strongest emotion he had was hate.

Hate for Christians.

Namir's first kill happened when he was eight years old.

It wasn't planned. His gun went off when he was playing with it and killed an old villager.

He fled the place and joined a wandering band of armed militants. War became not just his solace, but his profession.

The militants Namir had joined were a splinter group of Hezbollah, the group that had waged a political war, and sometimes terrorism, against Israel and America, and had persecuted people of other faiths.

Having grown up in a toxic environment, Namir quickly found he was better at military strategy than any other militant in his group. And that he liked killing and torture.

He also found he was uninterested in the ideological beliefs of the Hezbollah.

He killed the leader of his group when he was twenty-five. Took over the cell, which was fifty strong. Turned it into a Mafia-style gang and ruled over a small village in the Bekaa Valley.

Product and money. Only those two mattered. Religious killing, fanaticism, creating a caliphate—all that was of zero interest to him.

He still had a burning hatred for Christians. He killed them where he could.

However, he didn't allow his emotions to get in the way of his business.

The valley was broad and flat, a hundred miles northeast of Beirut, high up against the Anti-Lebanon Mountains. It had orchards, wineries, and factories for handmade carpets.

The village used to make wine at one time. Now it was better known for its hashish fields.

Namir's gang controlled hundreds of acres of such fields, the villagers effectively serving the bandits. Hashish sales, however, were being rapidly overtaken by the manufacture of Captagon, an addictive drug that helped fighters stay awake for days and fight like zombies.

Namir had converted four houses in the village into laboratories, the hub of his multimillion-dollar income.

It was when he turned thirty-five that it all came crashing down on him.

Chapter 2

He was returning from Beirut, where he and his men had killed twenty Christian men and raped the women with them. None had done anything to Namir or his gang.

The militants were on their way out of the city after being involved in an action against the Lebanese army. It had started raining, and their open-topped Jeeps didn't offer much protection.

They took cover in a church, where a group was praying. The occupants ordered them to leave.

Namir, high on Captagon, was in no mood to obey. His hatred for Christians surfaced.

He slapped the nearest man, at which several others from the church congregation rushed at him.

In no time, AKs slipped into the gang members' hands, and a few minutes later, many innocents were dead.

'We can have some fun,' one gunman said with a grin, looking in the direction of the women cowering in a corner of the church.

'Yes,' Namir agreed.

Unknown to him, one man had gotten away from the

massacre: Kenton Ashland, an American reporter.

Ashland had surreptitiously fled as the gunmen arrived. Hearing shots, he crept back to the doors of the church cautiously and hid beneath a vehicle parked in front of the wide-open doors. What he saw sickened him, and he started taking pictures and recording it on his cell.

He uploaded the images and video to the Internet, after which events moved quickly.

There were American forces in Beirut based close to the church. Some soldiers spotted the pictures, noted the time stamp and recognized the church.

They alerted their commander.

When Namir set out two hours later, a trap was ready, waiting.

The militants' capture was widely covered by international media, and Namir was branded a war criminal.

He was tried, amidst global publicity, in the Special Tribunal for Lebanon in the Netherlands. He was convicted and sentenced to fifteen years in prison.

He was transported back to Lebanon and began his jail time in Beirut.

However, he didn't serve his full term.

A month after his fortieth birthday, his gang members organized a full-scale attack on the prison, supported by others.

Namir escaped, along with several other prisoners.

He fled the country on a private plane after being provided with a fake passport and papers.

He went to Switzerland and got his face altered. Not by much, but enough to fool facial recognition programs.

He then flew to America using yet another passport.

Namir had a long memory. Coupled with that, he had an unforgiving nature.

It was time to pay Kenton Ashland a visit.

And bring war to anyone who stood in Namir's way.

Chapter 3

Zeb Carter feinted and slammed a fist into the rushing man's gut. The assailant wheezed but kept on coming.

Zeb had no room to maneuver. Behind him was the wall of the bar; in front of him were his attackers, three of them.

He went inside his attacker's punching range, took a blow to his shoulder, stiffened three fingers and jabbed them in the man's throat.

Sour breath washed over him as the goon choked, gasped, and gave up the fight.

The man's two friends then took up the attack.

They had held back, assuming their friend would sufficiently damage Zeb, but now, they came forward, their faces intent, their fists bunching.

Zeb shoved Sour Breath in their way, spun on his left heel, his right leg swinging up straight and hard as a concrete beam, and kicked the second aggressor on his shoulder.

The man staggered, a high keening sound emerging from his throat, as he clutched his shoulder and dropped to the ground.

That left the third man.

He was lean, wiry, narrow-faced. His eyes were watchful. There was none of his friends' rage on his face. He was cool, calculating.

'You can walk away,' Zeb told him, 'Before you get hurt.'

Wiry didn't reply. His eyes flicked over Zeb's shoulder, as if signaling someone behind.

Zeb didn't fall for that trick. He was watching the attacker's hands, which were hanging by his side.

Not a puncher, then. A shooter? A knife-man?

A soft *swish* answered his question as Wiry drew a wicked-looking blade from a thigh holster, and he stabbed forward.

Zeb evaded the flashing blade, mentally appreciating the move.

He's got some experience or training. That's a clean stab, not the wild waving most attackers display.

Wiry faked a move, and then slashed suddenly, almost catching Zeb by surprise.

The knife whistled through the air and sliced air an inch away from his throat.

Zeb let it pass, guessing there would be a second attack.

He guessed right.

The blade reversed, and instead of sweeping back, cut towards his face.

Now!

Wiry was leaning forward, his left hand dipping down, his stance open for a fraction.

Zeb surged forward, his head moving away from the slice, left fist punching the knife arm at the elbow, right palm coming up and crushing the attacker's throat.

He swiveled, his back turning, his hands sliding down the

knife hand, grabbing it, using his momentum to heave Wiry over his hip and send him crashing against the bar's wall.

A thin scream burst through the man before he slid down and lay motionless.

Zeb watched the three men for a moment. The first two were groaning and clutching their limbs. One of them had puked his guts out, the bitter smell carrying in the air.

Wiry rolled slowly to his knees, a hand scrabbling on the ground to find his knife. His head came up, baleful eyes staring at Zeb.

'You had a choice,' Zeb told him pitilessly. 'You could have stayed out.' He kneed him in the face and walked out into the darkness.

Chapter 4

Zeb was vacationing in the vastness of the Frank Church–River of No Return Wilderness in central Idaho: more than two million contiguous acres of rivers, mountains, dense forests and plains.

The Main Salmon River ran near the wilderness's northern boundary, and its canyon, six thousand three hundred feet deep, had earned it the name River of No Return.

The region was home to wolves, black bears, deer, elk, rattlesnakes and several other kinds of wildlife. What clinched it for Zeb was the scarcity of humans in the area.

He had set off from his hometown, New York, and driven across the Midwest and the northern states, and left his vehicle behind in Salmon, Idaho. He hiked into the wilderness for days until he found the largest ponderosa pines he'd seen, the farthest from any trails. And there he had set up camp.

Stanley, the nearest settlement, with a population of under seventy, was a good few hours' walk away. The spot couldn't have been more perfect.

There had been no missions for him at The Agency, the black-ops outfit he worked for. His crew, called the

Warriors in some circles, were on their downtime too. That had made it easy for him to get away and enjoy the company of the elements of the earth and the wildlife.

And then it had come crashing down, on the day of the fight.

The argument had started for no reason and played out like they did in old Westerns.

He had hiked to Stanley to stock up on supplies. There wasn't much to the town; there wouldn't be, with that size of population.

There was Eva Falls Avenue, which seemed to double as Main Street, with various establishments on each side of the street: a chamber of commerce, a post office, a hotel, a general store, and a few other buildings.

He bought what he needed at the store and, when the sun dipped behind the mountains, went to the solitary bar for a drink.

There were a few pick-up trucks in the parking lot and a gleaming red SUV with New York plates. He didn't pay it much attention as he headed inside.

There weren't many people inside: three men lined up against the small, dark wood counter—Wiry, Sour Breath, and their friend—a couple of men playing cards at a table, and an older man snoozing in a corner.

Zeb eased himself up to the bar, his shoulder brushing that of Sour Breath's.

The man muttered something unintelligible, turned his head to glare at Zeb, and reluctantly gave way.

Drunk, Zeb thought.

He ordered a freshly squeezed juice and heard a snigger from the three men.

'Juice,' Sour Breath mimicked and slapped his thigh in exaggerated laughter.

He turned when he felt Zeb's stare. 'What? You don't like a man-like drink?' he challenged.

'Mind your own business,' Zeb replied, curtly. He had a long hike ahead of him, in the dark, and was eager to get away.

'I would, if you didn't yell your order in my ear.'

'I didn't.'

'You did,' Sour Breath's face turned red.

The bartender returned with Zeb's drink and interrupted them.

Zeb would have normally taken his time, soaking up the ambience.

Not now.

He emptied his glass and was headed to the door when a hand grabbed his shoulder.

'I'm talking to you,' Sour Breath said, following him, his friends close behind.

'Buddy, I came here for a drink, just like you. Why don't you get back to enjoying your evening?'

'Not until you apologize.'

'And pay for our drinks,' the third man spoke up.

'Why would I do any of that?'

'Because you were rude,' Sour Breath said with a smirk.

Zeb looked him up and down and sized up his friends.

Nope, he hadn't seen them before. They seemed to be travelers. Their shoes were dusty, jeans stained. Their accents were unmistakable, from his state.

That SUV's theirs.

Nobody in the bar was paying them any attention. The bartender had disappeared, presumably to the kitchen, while the card-players were engrossed in their game. The sleeping man hadn't stirred.

Nope, can't be a setup. Not in the middle of nowhere in Idaho. No one knows who I am, here. No one other than my team knows where I am.

He shrugged off Sour Breath's hand and went swiftly to the door.

He was done talking. This was why he liked the wilderness. Blackbears and wolves didn't ask him to pay for their drinks.

The men followed him to the parking lot, which was to the side of the bar, and that was when Zeb knew they were angling for a fight.

Chapter 5

After dispatching the men, he crossed the street and, from the shadows of a shuttered building, watched them.

There was no movement for a long while, and then Wiry stumbled out under the single light shining on the bar's entryway.

He said something, and presently, Sour Breath and the third man came staggering out.

They stood swaying for a moment. Then two of them jumped back, cursing, when Sour Breath bent over and retched.

They grabbed him and hustled him to their vehicle, the SUV, swearing all their way.

Zeb drew out his phone and snapped their pictures. He noted the SUV's plate and waited till its red lights vanished in the night.

Then he set off for his camp.

His base was west of the Middle Fork Salmon River, a long distance from the Salmon Mountains to the west.

He reached it at one am and stood motionless against a ponderosa nearby, watching, listening.

There was a stream a couple of miles away, too far for him

to hear the rushing water.

The forest was quiet, but not utterly silent. Wind blew through it and trees sighed. Nightlife rustled in bushes.

No hostile presence, however. His radar didn't tingle.

He smiled wryly.

Just some tourists who had too much to drink.

He emerged from the canopy of trees and went to his dwelling, a crude hut fashioned from fallen logs, with a door woven from boughs and leaves. Strips of leather that he had carried with him to this spot served as hinges.

It had taken him three days of painstaking effort to build it, and he had loved every moment.

The floor of the hut was packed, hardened earth, and from its roof hung two battery-powered lanterns.

On the floor was a sleeping bag, and next to it his gear. A backpack that contained a spare Glock, ammo, a couple of knives, more combat and medical equipment, his screens and several battery packs. A larger bag held his hiking gear.

He removed his jacket and brought out one of his screens. He booted up his satellite phone to connect to Werner, the supercomputer in their Columbus Avenue office in New York. He ran the SUV's plates and put his photos of the men in the bar through a facial recognition program.

Werner responded quickly. None of the three was on any watchlist. Sour Breath was a store owner in the Bronx and had a few arrests for DUI, but nothing major. His friends were clean. One of them worked as a manager in a retail store, while the other was an insurance salesman.

No threat. Zeb shut down his devices and settled down to sleep.

The banging woke him up instantly, the Glock under his bag sliding into his palm as if by magic.

Three am, the dial on his wrist told him.

The door shuddered as someone pounded it again.

He turned off the lamps, plunging the room into darkness, stood to one side, and opened the door carefully.

His mouth opened in surprise when a figure stumbled inside, fell, and remained motionless.

He crouched down and froze.

It was a girl.

Young. He ran his eyes over her swiftly. No weapons.

She didn't look like she was a threat.

He snapped a glance outside. Nothing. No movement. No other person.

He left the hut and walked around in widening circles, alert, prepared.

He didn't come across anyone else.

He went back inside, and when he turned the lamps to full brightness, his insides clenched and a coldness gripped him.

The girl looked to be in her teens. Fourteen or fifteen years old, he guessed.

Her eyes were open, but she was clearly in shock.

He bent next to her, his lips tightening when he saw that her face and hands were scratched and bleeding. Her nails were muddy and a couple of them were torn.

He carried her gently—she was slim and didn't weigh much—to his sleeping bag. She began to mumble as he laid her down, a continuous stream of sound that made no sense to him initially.

He bent his ear to her mouth, and when he finally made out the words, he knew his vacation was over.

'Namir,' she said, 'He killed Dad. Many men. Behind me.'

Chapter 6

Several months earlier

Namir's escape had been planned, but not solely by his men.

The plan had been hatched when five men met in a remote village in the Bekaa. Each had arrived in a dusty vehicle filled with armed gunmen.

If American intelligence or any Western nation had known of the meeting, a drone would have blitzed the venue. Because the five were some of the most wanted men in the world.

However, Western intelligence wasn't aware of the meeting. Their satellites and drones were focused on the war in Raqqa. They had too much on their hands to pay any attention to a remote, lawless village in Lebanon.

The five were top commanders of ISIS who had fled to the Lebanese refuge, just over the Syrian border, once Raqqa, the terrorists' bastion, had been surrounded by the Syrian Democratic Forces.

The commanders had read the tea leaves; they knew what no terrorist dared to speak aloud.

ISIS was finished in Raqqa. Those who were captured would face a brutal end. They wouldn't receive Western justice. They would be lucky if their ending was swift and painless.

The eldest of them, Irfan Nawaf Safar, called the meeting to order. Their shooters had emptied the village and had ensured that their discussions wouldn't be overheard.

'Any news?' the youngest leader, Ishaq Ghanem, asked before Safar could speak another word.

Safar's face turned bleak as he shook his head. 'There is no radio contact, but you know what's happening. We are finished in Raqqa. The Americans and the SDF have won.'

'What about the Supreme Leader?'

Safar's lips thinned, his face closed, 'He is alive, well. That's all anyone needs to know.'

'That's it? We give up?' Ghanem asked angrily.

He flushed when Safar's eyes turned dark and zeroed in on him.

'I mean, do we have any plans to hit back?' he mumbled apologetically.

Safar weighed him for a long while. The young commander had risen fast because he had smarts. He could think strategically and was ruthless; the two qualities didn't often go together.

'Why do you think I called this meeting?' he said, smiling grimly when the others leaned forward in anticipation.

'Where? How? We hit them in Raqqa? From behind?' One of them asked.

'In Mosul. Let's go there,' another argued.

'Let's attack in Turkey,' yet another chimed in.

Safar held up a hand to silence them.

'Do you know why our attacks are successful?'

'No one can predict them,' the four answered as one.

'Yes, but if we want to make their people feel really scared, where do we hit them?'

'London or America,' Ghanem answered promptly.

Chapter 7

Safar nodded. 'That's right. But London has already been attacked this year. We need a new target.'

'America,' Ghanem's eyes lit up. Rubbing his hands together unconsciously, he said: 'I will lead it.'

A disturbance at the door interrupted Safar before he could reply. His head rose angrily when a fighter entered the room unannounced.

'Shall I bring lunch, sayidi?' the man stammered.

The older leader relaxed and nodded.

The five commanders waited until their food had been served, a simple meal of lamb and rice with water to wash it down.

Safar wiped his lips when their plates had been cleared and they were alone again. 'We need a crazed killer. Someone who is capable of doing anything.'

His eyes glittered. 'Because this attack will have no rules. Our killer will have all the freedom to select his targets.'

'All our attacks are like that,' one of the men protested.

'Yes, but this will be like a series of attacks. Across America.'

'Like a serial killer on the loose?' one man asked stupidly.

Safar stared at him balefully. 'We are terrorists, not serial killers.'

Ghanem snapped his fingers excitedly, 'You mean our man will move from place to place, killing randomly?'

'Yes. Everyone will know these are terrorist attacks. But no one will know when the next one is coming, or where.'

'Isn't that dangerous?' one of the leaders shifted uneasily. 'Our man will be caught sooner or later.'

'Not if we plan it right. It's not as if the attacks will continue for months. Just a couple of days. Each one will be violent. They will be spectacular. Our flag will be left at each site.'

He looked around at the men facing him and could sense their excitement, their eagerness.

Each of them had drawn blood in war. They had killed innocents as well as soldiers. They had tortured and raped.

Their ability to kill in cold blood was one reason they had risen to the top of ISIS's ranks.

'This one will be in the remote parts of America. Where everyone thinks they are safe. That will make them realize they will never be safe as long as we are alive.'

'I want to be that killer,' Ghanem breathed, his face alight. 'I want to go to America and wreak such savagery on them that they will never forget. You know I can do it.'

Safar regarded him for a moment. Yes, Ghanem was capable of such terror. But he wasn't who the elder man had in mind.

'I heard you the first time,' he told Ghanem sternly. 'It will be none of us. The killer will be someone not associated with us.'

'Who, then?'

'Namir.'

Chapter 8

It took some time for Safar to convince the remaining commanders of his choice.

'He's Hezbollah. Shia. They are our enemies. Why should we use him? We have our own killers,' Ghanem responded furiously.

'He *was* Hezbollah. Everyone knows he hates Christians. He doesn't care about any other religion. Shia, Sunni, that doesn't matter to him. And that's why he is perfect. He is ruthless. He is vicious. He is interested only in money. And no one will suspect he is our man,' Safar retorted.

He spent another hour outlining his case, at the end of which his fellow commanders were on board.

Events moved rapidly after that. Namir's men were approached, and secretive discussions began.

Namir himself was reached in prison. The Lebanese jail was a highly secure one, but finding prisoners sympathetic to ISIS wasn't difficult. There were such people in every corner of the world. The prisoners conveyed an oblique message to Namir, who understood it immediately.

He signed up promptly.

Hezbollah and ISIS didn't see eye to eye and had fought each other in Syria, but to Namir all that didn't matter.

He had broken away from Hezbollah and formed his own cell, hadn't he? He was a drug warlord. He wasn't into feudal warfare.

Getting out of prison? Going to America to kill? Freedom to choose his targets? He would be a free operator once he escaped from prison.

What was there to debate?

So what if it was planned by ISIS? So what that they had threatened to hunt him down if he didn't carry out his killings in America?

He knew the threat was genuine and that the terrorist organization had long arms.

He also knew he was being used by ISIS. However, none of that mattered.

He had planned to go to America in any case, once he had served his time. The ISIS plan meant that he would be going to the Great Satan sooner rather than later. He could pursue his own agenda.

It all tied up neatly.

He had planned a meeting in America. That meeting could now become part of the ISIS agenda of killing.

'I am in,' he replied through the prison pipeline, and began making plans.

ISIS wanted vicious, crazed killings?

He would give them that.

But his meeting would come first.

With Kenton Ashland.

The jailbreak was spectacular, and Namir couldn't help

smirking when his name lit up TV screens around the world.

He strutted when he heard that he was the most-wanted man on the planet.

He sneered and smiled all the way to America. He chuckled when he crossed immigration control at the airport with ease. For all its boasts, America's border control was surprisingly easy to fool.

It helped that ISIS had come up with a master plan.

The passports and the papers he and his men were carrying identified them as Saudi businessmen. They were coming to America, bringing their oil money to invest in businesses.

Namir's chuckle turned to a grin when the burly officer stamped his passport and waved him inside the country.

The Americans had no idea they had just admitted their most dangerous enemy.

Chapter 9

Present Day

Zeb wasn't sure he heard the name right. He listened carefully to the girl mumble.

She said Namir. No doubt about it.

He knew that name well. Hell, the whole world knew. TV and newspapers had milked the terrorist's escape for days.

Every law enforcement agency was on the lookout for the dreaded terrorist, but he seemed to have dropped off the Earth.

He observed the girl closely as he wiped her face with a soft towel dipped in warm water. He cleaned the cuts on her hands.

None was severe. Youth and nature would heal the wounds.

She had brown eyes. Brown hair. Standard teenage attire of hoodie and T-shirt.

Nails short and unlacquered. Jeans, socks and sneakers completed her attire.

The bleeding on her face appeared to be from scratches, not from an assault, as he had initially feared.

There were traces of leaves and branches in her hair, and

he removed them as best he could.

He attempted to rouse her but gave up when she didn't respond.

He zipped her up in his sleeping bag to ease her shivering and went back to his screen.

Werner replied promptly at his commands.

No mention or sighting of Namir in the United States. The terrorist was still at large. Law enforcement agencies the world over were watchful.

If she's right, how did he get into the country?

He discarded the thought immediately. There were several ways to get past immigration officers in any country.

I should know. I use fake documents all the time.

He looked at his sat phone and thought about making a call to Clare, his boss.

Nope. She too has taken a rare vacation. Let her enjoy it.

Broker and Sarah Burke, his girlfriend, were in the Bahamas. Bwana, Roger, and their girlfriends were in France. Bear and Chloe were in India, while the Petersens were in Switzerland.

Every one of them would cancel their holidays without a second thought if they thought he needed them.

Hell, they'll come running, locked and loaded, ready for a fight, if they even suspect I am in a jam.

He wasn't going to call them. He would deal with the girl by himself.

She's in shock. She might have misheard that name.

He dimmed the lamps and went outside the hut, listening carefully.

Nothing came to his ears.

He did a perimeter check. All good.

He went inside and looked at the girl. She had stopped her muttering, and her eyes were closed.

He went closer and heard her soft breathing. Sleeping.

That should help her.

He couldn't forget what she'd said, however.

She might have got Namir's name wrong, but what about her dad's killing? No child will say that.

He turned on the small gas stove and heated water for tea, as his mind raced through possibilities.

He was pouring the drink into two plastic cups when a voice spoke from behind him.

'Who are you?'

Chapter 10

He filled the cups before turning around. She was sitting up now, propped up by her left hand.

Her eyes were suspicious, her body tense, but it was what she was gripping in her right hand that drew his attention.

His spare Glock.

He slept with two of them underneath his sleeping bag. One gun was on him; the other was now with her.

He was struck by the easy familiarity with which she held the gun. Her palm curved around its butt firmly, its barrel unwavering as it pointed towards him.

'I am Zeb Carter. I am a hiker,' he replied calmly.

Defuse the situation first.

Her eyes moved around the hut. They rested for a moment on his backpacks, lingered on the screen and sat phone on top of his smaller bag, and returned to him when she had finished her survey.

'You made this yourself?' she pointed the gun at the roof.

'This hut? Yeah.'

'Cool.'

He frowned inwardly. Cool wasn't the word a girl would

have used. Not if her father had been killed. Not if she was hunted by Namir, or anyone else.

'How did you find me?' she interrupted his thinking.

'You found me. You came to my hut.'

And then her memory seemed to return.

Her eyes widened. The Glock dropped. Her lips trembled.

'My God,' she whispered. 'He killed Dad ... Dad.' She bent double, retching, dry heaves that wracked her small body.

He dropped the tea cups and rushed forward to hold her.

'No, no,' she screamed, her fists pounding against his chest. 'You are one of them. You killed my father. You are Namir's man.'

'No. I am not one of them.' He held her closer, smothering her fight till he felt her shudder and start sobbing, her tears dampening his T-shirt.

'Let me go,' she screamed and bit his shoulder hard.

He winced but didn't release her.

'Listen,' he told her, blinking to ward off the pain. 'If I was one of them, you would already be dead.'

She didn't respond, but her wriggling lessened, and then stopped.

She stiffened suddenly.

'They are coming.' Her face went white, her head bobbing wildly as she searched the room in panic.

'No one is here,' he comforted her. 'No one is outside. I checked. What do you mean, Namir killed your father? How do you know Namir?'

She wrenched out of his grasp, 'We have no time for this,' she shouted, fear and rage lacing her voice. 'His men were chasing me. They are not far behind. Dad ... what they did to him ...'

She bolted for the door and fled into the night.

Chapter 11

Zeb stood stock-still for a moment, taken aback by her sudden move.

There was a time I was good with children.

He buried the thought, grabbed his jacket, armored vest, his sat phone, the spare Glock and the mags underneath the sleeping bag, and hurried outside.

No sign of her.

'You there?' he called out softly.

'They are coming,' he heard her sob from the forest. 'They will kill me. Like they killed Dad.'

Her voice helped him get her bearings. She was behind the hut, running away.

She was heading toward the canyon half a mile away.

Canyon!

He set off at a run, cursing himself.

The canyon was some distance away, but closer to his camp was a deep fissure in the ground, twenty feet wide and several feet deep.

Following long-practiced habit, he had deliberately set his camp near it, to reduce the chance of a surprise attack from the rear.

Now, it played against him. An opening of that size would easily swallow the girl.

He had posted signs on trees to warn other hikers.

But she won't see them. She is frightened. Terrified.

He upped his pace, ignoring branches and boughs slapping at his face.

She had just a few minutes on him, but it felt like hours.

He heard her at last, above the sound of his own breathing, as she thrashed, crying loudly, praying.

Praying.

His heart clenched. He swerved past a giant ponderosa and spotted her shadow.

She heard him approaching and turned a fear-stricken face toward him.

'Nooo, don't stop me,' she cried and ran faster

She is beyond reasoning. I can't convince her.

He saw one of his signs flash past, on a tree. *She's not far from that crack.*

Zeb dove headlong, his hands outspread.

They curled around her and grabbed her as he landed, rolled on his shoulder, and came to rest just a few feet away from the void in the ground.

'Stop,' he spoke, above her muffled screams as she kicked and punched him. 'Look over my shoulder. There's a hole in the ground. You would have fallen in it.'

Her struggling ebbed. She turned her face up to peer over him and shuddered when she saw the chasm, dark against the moonlit earth, running behind them in a jagged line.

'It is so deep that you would have injured yourself. Maybe gotten killed. I had to stop you.'

He could feel her heart thumping against his chest. Her rapid breathing fanned his ears.

A memory stirred and came to the surface.

His arms hugging a small body.

His hands tightened a fraction around the girl.

And a shot rang out.

Chapter 12

———∞∞∞———

He snapped his head up.

That wasn't aimed at us. No round striking anywhere near us.

He shushed her as she started trembling, and strained to hear over her breathing.

'It's them,' she gulped, 'I told you they would come.'

He raised a finger to silence her and listened carefully. He thought he heard the distant sounds of men but couldn't be sure. The report had come from beyond his hut, but in the same direction.

He rose smoothly, caught her left hand in his, his Glock in his right.

'Follow me,' he whispered. 'Don't make a sound.'

He started back to his camp, but she tugged back.

'They'll be there.' Her lip quivered, but her eyes were fierce. 'They want me.'

'My gear is back there. We have to get it.'

'You don't know them.' A tear rolled down her face. 'I saw what they did to Dad. They made me watch.'

I know many men like that. It's my job to exterminate them.

'We will be careful,' he promised.

'Why should I trust you?'

He regarded her for a long moment. For such a teenager, she displayed a surprising maturity. Her language, her diction, even her composure, despite what she had witnessed, was that of an adult.

'Because they will kill me, too.'

'Why do you have two Glocks?'

'Later. We need to go back quickly.'

He walked fast, hastily but not recklessly. He let his chi spread out and act like a radar.

He ghosted around trees and slid through head-high bushes.

She followed without complaint, grabbing his hand tightly.

He counted the distance in his mind, alert for any shadows in the darkness. Any unusual movement.

He slowed and then came to a stop when they neared his camp, approaching the hut from the side.

He stopped behind a thicket and, using it as cover, watched.

There was a lightening in the darkness ahead of them. Probably a hundred yards away. Close to where his camp was.

The forest blocked any view, but they could hear voices. Several of them.

She threw a wide-eyed look at him. He nodded in as reassuring a manner as he could and dropped to his knees.

It was time to crawl.

They made their way slowly until they came within sighting distance of his hut.

He swallowed bitterly at the scene in front of him.

Several men were crowded in front of the house, too far away to make out their individual details. But he recognized the angular shapes in their hands.

Every one of them was armed.

Chapter 13

One of them probably fired at the house. Which was what we heard.

A shout came from inside the house as they watched. A man came running out, holding something in his hand.

He headed to a tall man in the center of the group. Zeb could make out a beard on the central man's face. There was something about his stance, the way the other men spread out around him.

The leader? Namir?

Tall Man inspected what his shooter was holding and rapped out orders.

What is it? She didn't leave anything behind. Her hoodie is on her. Her sneakers, too.

His heart sank when he remembered.

He had snipped away a few strands of her long hair as he had cleaned her up.

Those hairs were next to the sleeping bag. She escaped before I could clean up. Before I could do anything.

Another man came out of the house, his arms full.

Zeb's fingers tightened when he recognized his screens,

his spare phone, and the battery packs.

A bow-legged shooter exited the hut, carrying Zeb's backpacks, and dumped them at Tall Man's feet.

The leader rapped out questions as he kicked at the bags.

His men shook their heads.

One of them handed a screen over to him. He pressed buttons, fiddled with it, and threw it to the ground.

Zeb couldn't help smiling.

His screens and his phones had biometric protection. They wiped themselves clean the moment they were handled by strangers.

His backpacks had no identification on them.

They won't know who I am.

But my problem is bigger. I have nothing on me other than my Glocks and some ammo. And the sat phone.

That reminded him. He withdrew his phone and snapped several photographs of the men.

He counted twenty-one. He took as many pictures as he could, of each one.

He then turned on the phone's recorder and pointed it in the direction of the men.

Maybe it could pick up what they were saying. There were software programs that could eliminate noise and enhance the voice quality.

Tall Man went inside the hut, two men accompanying him. Returning, he placed his hands on his hips and rotated slowly, looking at the forest around him.

Zeb felt the girl shrink instinctively when the leader looked their way.

Tall Man then made an unmistakable sign. A circling

motion with his hand that meant, *search the forest.*
'What do we do now?' the girl asked him despairingly.
'We run.'

Chapter 14

Earlier

The first thing Namir felt needed to happen on arriving in America was getting his men to shave. Not totally, however. Going hairless wasn't the plan.

Namir got them to trim their beards and get neat haircuts. He insisted on their wearing clean, Western clothes, to look as if they belonged.

Appearances mattered.

The second item on the agenda was weaponing up. ISIS helped him in that.

He received a single text message on the throwaway phone he'd bought.

The message consisted of a name, Asif Iqbal, and an address in Texas.

Namir knew ISIS was also sending a covert message through that text: that they could find him wherever he was.

He wasn't bothered. He would carry out the killing spree his masters desired.

After executing Kenton Ashland.

He rented four vehicles, and the group set off for Texas from New York. None had driven in America, and the interstate highways took some getting used to.

A couple of his men couldn't help staring at American women in their short skirts. Namir tore a strip off their butts with his tongue, and from then on, they behaved.

No Arabic: that was another rule he insisted on. Everyone would speak in English, however broken it was. He was fluent enough in English, and in any case, their cover as Saudis would explain their lack of proficiency.

Asif Iqbal's address turned out to be a rundown trucking warehouse in an industrial park outside Houston, in a corner all by itself.

Metal was peeling off its shutters. The few trucks in the lot were old.

Namir watched the warehouse for a full day. He scattered the group's vehicles behind several trucks and rotated his men on surveillance duty.

He personally inspected all the parked vehicles on the street.

There were no police cruisers. No vehicles with antennae sticking out.

The industrial park looked like it had business-as-usual traffic. One building was occupied by an office supplies company; another, a bathroom fittings manufacturer.

Normal businesses, with normal-looking staff. Some pudgy, some lean, women, men, black, white. A mix that reflected the country's melting pot.

Once he was sure there was no trap set, no cops in waiting, he approached the warehouse.

Iqbal looked to be in his thirties. He had a scrawny neck, a straggly beard that fell over a soiled T-shirt. His dirty jeans stank.

His brown eyes flicked over Namir's men and then to the cellphone the terrorist presented to him.

'No names,' he snapped after reading the text message. 'I don't want to know who you are. Or what you intend to do.'

His attitude grated on Namir. He thought of snapping Iqbal's neck.

'I plan to kill you.'

Chapter 15

Namir smiled mirthlessly when Iqbal sprang back in alarm.

'If you don't give me weapons,' Namir clarified and displayed his teeth when the trucker swore.

Iqbal had plenty of weapons.

Namir's eyes popped in disbelief when he saw the array of guns in the warehouse the cell owned.

Iqbal's trucking company turned out to be a five-man cell that stood ready to outfit people like Namir: ISIS killers.

The warehouse had all kinds of weapons: HKs, Sig Sauers, Remingtons, M16s, they were all available.

Namir selected HK MP7s as their main assault weapons, and Sig Sauers for handguns. He stocked up on ammo and knives.

'Secure phones?' he asked the cell leader.

Iqbal disappeared inside the warehouse and returned with a carton.

He ripped it open and brought out a collection of smartphones.

'Not those,' Namir said, tossed them aside. 'Older models. Much older models.'

Iqbal brought out devices that had nothing much on them

but keypads. All in black.

'Namir grunted in satisfaction. 'Jammers?'

'Those are hard to get.'

'Get them.'

Iqbal got them the next day, a whole carton full, and he added a bonus.

'Satellite phone jammers,' he announced proudly as he held up another box containing two box-like devices. 'They have a two-hundred-meter radius and can jam any signal: cell, GPS, or sat phone.'

Namir fingered the equipment and sat back in his chair. 'Show me,' he ordered.

Iqbal leaped up and plugged one of the jammers into a power socket. He fiddled with dials and then inserted SIM cards into two phones.

'Make a call,' he said, tossing one to Namir.

Namir dialed the number Iqbal read out, and held the cell to his ear.

No response.

'See?' Iqbal grinned. 'They work. Those babies are new. We paid big bucks to secure them. They are military grade.'

Namir made no response. He looked at two of his men, who nodded silently.

They rose and went to the warehouse doors. They rolled them shut and closed the rear exit as well.

'What's up, dude?' Iqbal asked in confusion.

'This,' Namir replied, and shot him and the rest of the sleeper cell members.

'You wiped out the entire cell!' Safar screamed at him that evening, over a secure Internet call on a laptop.

Namir was in a motel, in a room all to himself. The computer was a used one he had bought and the call was through a messaging service—protocols he had agreed to after his escape from prison.

'They saw our faces,' he replied, unapologetically.

'Anyone who can identify me, in this country, in your network, dies.'

Chapter 16

Finding Kenton Ashland proved easier than he anticipated.

Namir searched for him randomly on the Internet, and there he was.

The journalist was in Erilyn, a small town in Idaho, population 2,000. He was chief editor for The Erilyn Tribune, the local weekly.

He went to the newspaper's website and clicked on Ashland's bio.

His blood pounded as he read that the journalist was highly respected. He had received several awards for his reporting. The president had awarded him some kind of medal for his role in putting away Namir.

The terrorist slammed his laptop shut and rose.

He got a medal for putting me in prison.
I will see just how brave he is.

When he'd calmed down, he looked up Erilyn.

It was a small dot on the map close to something called the Frank Church Wilderness. The town was not far from the Montana state line, and south of the Canadian border.

He lay on his bed, thinking. The journalist could have had a job in any large city. Why Erilyn?

He went back to the newspaper's site and, in an archived story, found his answer.

In an interview, Ashland had said he wanted to bring up Sara Ashland, his daughter, in a small town. In the same place where his father lived.

Namir searched some more, but there were no other details on Ashland's family.

It didn't matter. Family or no family, Kenton Ashland was a dead man walking.

It took three days to get from Houston to Erilyn. From the south of America to its north.

As he drove, Namir began to realize how vast the country was. Miles of nothingness would pass, as their vehicles drove over blacktop.

In the distance, there would be a farmhouse, surrounded by fields of wheat or some other crop.

There would be large swathes of barren land before a town appeared.

There was traffic. Large eighteen-wheelers that trundled past them, occasionally sounding their horns.

On the evening of the third day, after Namir rented a new set of wheels, they rolled into Erilyn.

On the fourth day, he spotted Ashland.

The journalist was in a coffee store, seated with another man, laughing, as Namir walked past.

The town wasn't large. It had a Main Street, from which several branches sprang. Most of the houses were on the smaller lanes.

Main Street had a few banks, a few grocery stores and hotels, and it had the newspaper office.

Namir was strolling on the pavement when he saw the journalist. He recognized him immediately.

The same reddish beard, the same green eyes. Ashland hadn't changed.

He liked the color of the journalist's hair.

It will match the color of his blood. Once I spill it.

Chapter 17

Now that his prey was in sight, Namir carried out his plan.

He distributed his men in various motel rooms. They were tourists, exploring the country; that was their cover.

He took a room close to the newspaper office and went about trailing Ashland.

The journalist lived on Elm Street, in a red-brick house set back from the street by a generous front yard.

He and his teenaged daughter lived alone. She shared none of his features. Her brown hair and brown eyes bore no resemblance to his.

Each day, Ashland walked her to school a couple of blocks away.

The journalist then carried on to his office, where he spent the majority of his day. Sometimes he came out for a coffee. Or to meet someone.

In the evening, he collected his daughter from school and walked back home.

Everyone knew the editor. People greeted him on the street, stopped him to shake his hand, or slapped his back.

On Sundays, Ashland and his daughter went to church.

It was a tall building, imposing with its red-brick walls and white tower. It had an air of serenity about it, and induced people to talk softly as they entered it.

The building was packed for Sunday worship. Namir counted a hundred people entering it—*a hundred infidels*, he corrected himself—as he discreetly observed from his vehicle.

A plan started forming in Namir's head as he watched the journalist emerge from the building, cracking a joke with his daughter.

'You are not keeping contact,' Safar growled over the Internet that evening.

'Which is good,' Namir snapped back. 'You promised me I would be a lone operator. What do you want?'

'What progress have you made?'

Namir rocked back in his chair in anger. 'You thought I would come here, pick up guns, and start shooting randomly? You think I am a fool?

'They call me Namir for a reason,' he said, spittle spraying his screen. 'I am smart. I make plans. I don't strike blindly. You want to know progress? Watch the news every day.'

He cut the connection and grinned. The anger was an act. He had no intention of letting ISIS know of his plans.

They don't care if I die here. Well, I have no intention of becoming a martyr.

He wiped his computer off and researched the town. He measured the distance to the Canadian border, a stretch that seemed sparsely populated. That would be his escape route.

He checked out the police presence in Erilyn.

A chief of police and fewer than ten officers, housed in a building in a side street. Nowhere close to the church.

Kill Ashland. Send some men to attack the police station and distract them.

I will lead the rest to church.

Not to pray. To massacre.

Chapter 18

Namir got a break on Monday. He was in the coffee shop, a couple of seats behind Ashland and close enough to overhear his conversation with another man.

They were talking of deadlines and scoops.

And then the question that perked up his ears.

'You are all set for your camping trip? To Frank Church?'

'Yeah,' Ashland laughed. 'Sara's looking forward to it. She talks of nothing else. She's planned everything. Where we will camp. Hike. What we'll do for food.'

'You're going tomorrow?'

'Yes, and back on Saturday. In time for Sunday service.'

The men rose when Ashland paid the check, and left the café.

Namir didn't follow. His mind was whirling.

This is it. This is my chance.

He rushed to his room and researched the wilderness, then called his men and briefed them.

They would follow Ashland wherever he went.

The forest was ideal for what he planned.

'More than two million acres?' one of his men said, his mouth agape.

'Yes. No one will hear him scream.'

He bought camping gear for his men in the afternoon and rented four fresh SUVs, different colors so they wouldn't look like a single group.

At dawn Tuesday, Namir was parked on Ashland's street, a few houses away, waiting.

The girl tumbled out the door at nine am, turned around and beckoned her father.

Ashland came out presently, lugging two large backpacks.

He dumped them in a red SUV parked on the street. High-fived his daughter, went back to the house, locked it, and returned.

They left shortly afterward, unaware that death was following them.

Ashland drove southwest for three hours and finally parked his vehicle in a large trailhead lot at the edge of the forest.

Namir, leading his convoy, hung back, idling just out of sight while waiting for the pair to unpack their gear and begin walking into the forest. Once they had disappeared down the trail, he parked quickly and motioned for his men to follow.

They unpacked their gear swiftly and followed.

They could hear the girl's laughter in the distance, her voice guiding them as they walked. When the Ashlands stopped for lunch, Namir and his men stopped, too.

Looking back over his shoulder at his men, Namir felt proud of their discipline. Following him single-file, they carried their weapons openly, now that there was no one around.

They made no sound. No crude jokes. All of them intent on their mission.

At six pm, Ashland halted in a clearing.

'Here?'

'Yes.' Sara bounced up and down, holding a hand-drawn map. 'Right here. The trees are behind us. You can hear a stream if you are quiet. Get to work, Dad.'

Ashland pitched their tent and unfolded their sleeping bags inside. He hung two lanterns, and placed the gas stove in front of the tent.

He put a pot of water on it and was lighting it when he heard footsteps.

A man came out of the treeline, straight toward him.

He was wearing a hat, with shades pushed back on his head. He was armed.

Behind him, more men emerged.

Ashland got to his feet. Armed men were not uncommon in the wilderness.

'Hello, Kenton. It has been a long time.'

RUN!

Part II

Chapter 19

Present day

Namir kicked the ground in rage.

One girl. One little slip of a girl had evaded them.

'Find her. Find who is with her. Bring both back. Alive,' he yelled.

'Stop,' he roared when his men started scattering. 'Not all of you, you fools. Six of you stay back. The rest, go.'

His men broke up into four groups and went in four directions: one behind the house, another to its east, a third group to the west, and the last to the front.

'What are you waiting for?' He challenged the six remaining men. 'Go inside that hut. Find out who that person is. *I need a name.*'

He stared broodingly at the light coming out of the shelter as his men ripped it apart.

Subduing Ashland hadn't taken much effort.

The journalist had been slack-jawed when Namir introduced himself, but had quickly dived to his backpack.

'Sara. RUN!' he had yelled in despair as two of Namir's gunmen pounced on him. A third man chased the girl as she fled, caught her, and brought her back.

Namir would never forget how the first cut had felt. How the blade had sunk into Ashland. The way he had screamed.

He had tortured him slowly as his daughter cried and prayed.

Namir had laughed. He was judge, jury, and executioner. He was God.

And then, when everyone's attention was on Namir and his knife, the girl had taken action: kicked her captor in the groin and escaped.

Namir hadn't even turned around. He was intent on seeing the light die out in Ashland's eyes.

When his blood lust was sated, he found his men had returned empty-handed.

Sara Ashland was gone.

Zeb watched for a few moments longer.

Three men were heading in their direction. Flashlights in one hand, guns in the other. Heads looking down.

There was another bunch of three men and two groups of four, spreading out.

He caught the girl's hand and felt her shake.

He looked down and pressed his finger to his lips.

Started easing back, still facing the men. One step at a time. Feet rolling on the ground, distributing weight evenly. The way animals moved.

She followed.

The men merged into the shadows, and then they moved faster until they reached a dense copse.

He let his eyes adjust to the deeper gloom. It was a natural hollow surrounded by trees.

It would do.

He hurried her inside.

'Stay here. Don't move,' he whispered.

'Where are you going?' She forced the question through chattering teeth.

'To get us a gun.'

Chapter 20

She pulled him back, her eyes pleading.

He crouched in front of her.

'I won't be long. Less than ten minutes. Trust me.'

Her eyes were dark pools of fear, her lips white. She looked at him as if she could read him. Then nodded shakily.

He left swiftly. Ghosting from tree to tree. Breathing shallowly. Letting the beast in him rise and take over.

Letting his awareness cast a net around him.

Fifteen minutes later, he heard the crack of a twig.

He took cover behind a pine tree, feeling its bark scrape against his cheek.

It smelled earthy. Clean. He peered around it slowly.

They were coming from his left. A trajectory that would take them away from the copse. Away from him.

Single file. One behind the other.

Their lights playing in front of them. Short bursts of whispers between them.

Zeb waited till the undergrowth hid them and then moved.

He picked up some loose gravel. Followed them until he could hear their movements.

The last man came into sight, separated from the others by ten feet.

Zeb tossed a pebble to the left.

The killer froze. He didn't call out to his friends. Just like Zeb had guessed.

No one calls out at the first sound. It could turn out to be innocuous.

The ten foot gap became fifteen.

The killers at the front were now out of sight.

Zeb's target pointed his light at the sound.

All he saw was masses of bushes and small trees.

He was turning to leave when Zeb struck.

The butt of his Glock crashed into the gunman's temple.

His arm snaked around the shooter's neck. His left leg kicked out the man's legs.

Squeeze. Strike. Squeeze. Strike.

The man thrashed, his feet and hands flailing, trying to reach behind him.

Zeb was remorseless. He kept pounding and suffocating, and tightened his grip when the man groaned inaudibly.

'Abbas!' a voice called out from far ahead.

Zeb dragged his man into the deep forest.

'Abbas.'

Footsteps pounded. A gun chattered. Shots went off blindly, seeking a target. One that didn't exist.

Zeb was nowhere near the deadly rounds.

He was hugging the ground as the body next to him twitched and went still.

He could hear Abbas's friends argue. And then their sounds faded.

He looked at the body next to him. Felt nothing. A parasite had been terminated.

One man down.

Chapter 21

The girl was almost in shock when he returned, carrying Abbas's possessions. His HK MP7, his cellphone, his water canteen and his power bars, and his wallet.

She gasped loudly in relief when she saw him and fell into his arms.

He held her until her trembling had lessened and then rose.

'We have to go.'

'Where?' she asked tremulously.

'Deeper into the forest.'

Away from the Middle Fork River. Toward the mountains.

He set off at a fast pace, using the dim light to guide him, confident that none of the killers would return.

They will not hunt now. Not in the darkness, when they have already lost a man. They will resume in the morning. When daylight is on their side.

When the girl was close to exhaustion, he carried her. She was light, frail; she soon fell asleep, lulled by his movement.

His pace was brutal and would have exhausted ordinary men.

Five miles later, he came across two fallen trees, both

rotting, with a pile of dead leaves and branches collected around them.

He started to go around them, then changed his mind and looked beneath.

The tree behind was resting at an angle, the wide base of it propped on a rocky outcrop.

He laid the girl down gently and thrust a hand underneath the trunk.

The space was roomy. Large enough to comfortably shelter her.

He cleaned the opening, made a bed of soft leaves, and woke her up.

'That's your mattress.'

She looked at him heavy-lidded and then at the tree trunk.

She crawled underneath without a word and within seconds was fast asleep.

He covered her with his jacket and lay down in front of her.

Zeb woke at six am. Streaks of sunlight were streaming down the thick canopy overhead, brightening the forest.

He lay motionless, checking out his surroundings.

Trees as far as he could see. The sounds of birds. A chopper hovering somewhere far away, then fading.

He rose, found rain water in a hollow and washed his face, and returned.

'Who *are* you?'

Her voice stopped him as he was inspecting Abbas's possessions, the terrorist's HK MP7 slung around his shoulder.

All he could see were the whites of her eyes as she lay beneath the trunk.

'Zeb Carter. A hiker. I told you.'

'I don't believe you. My dad and I camped a lot. We met many hikers. Not one was like you.'

'Who are you?' he countered.

'Sara Ashland,' she replied after a long pause. 'Dad was Kenton Ashland.'

Chapter 22

The name rang a distant bell, but he didn't place it immediately.

'Kenton Ashland,' he rolled it around his tongue. 'I think I have heard it before.'

'You would have,' she said as she crawled out from underneath the trunk and went to where he was pointing, the small pool.

She cleaned her face, rinsed her mouth, and drank from the canteen of water he thrust at her.

Abbas's canteen. Which the killer no longer needed.

'If you followed the news,' she said, finally completing the thought, 'Dad was a famous journalist. It was his video and testimony that put Namir away.'

It came back to him. He recollected the news reports he had followed. The Agency dossiers on the terrorist's escape, arrest, and subsequent trial.

'He swore he would get Dad. He did.' She started shivering again, her eyes hollow, empty of any hope.

'What happened?'

'We came camping yesterday. From Erilyn, where we live.

The plan was to stay here till Saturday, return in the evening.'

He gave her a jacket. She draped it around herself, without any questions.

Abbas's jacket.

'Namir came in the evening. I was helping Dad set up the tent, the stove.'

She sniffed and wiped her eyes on her sleeve.

Something about her accent. Her looks.

He looked away and closed his eyes, hearing her words. Thought about the way she rolled some vowels and accentuated syllables.

'"Hello, Kenton," he said,' she recalled, crying softly, 'before torturing him.'

Zeb made no move to go closer to her. She had a remote look about her, despite her tears.

Grief. Shock. Anger. Fear. She's trying to process all of them.

'He cut Dad …' A gut-wrenching moan escaped her. She fell to her knees and hugged herself, swaying, giving up all pretense of holding it in.

He let her cry. He let her bawl and rage, her screams lost in the wilderness

'How did you escape?' he asked her when she was all cried-out and had gotten up to wash her face again.

'I kneed him, the man holding me, in the groin. Dad was close to …'

'You are Iraqi,' he interrupted her. 'You are Yazidi.'

'How did you know?' she asked in surprise.

'Your accent. I've been trying to place it. Then, your looks.'

'Just who are you, Mr. Carter?'

He fumbled in his pocket and drew out his sat phone, lifting a finger to stop her questions.

No signal.

He frowned and looked at its screen.

Tried again.

The same result.

He brought out Abbas's cell, fumbled with his sat phone and dropped it.

As he was bending to retrieve it, he saw a diving eagle abruptly change direction.

Move!

He lunged forward and grabbed her.

Raced deeper inside the forest, ignoring her squawk of surprise.

Just as a couple of men came into view.

And fired in their direction.

Chapter 23

Escape!

Desperation gave flight to their feet.

They flew through the forest, Zeb leading and dragging her behind him.

Swerving through trees. Zigzagging.

Rounds slapping into trunks, shredding branches, ripping through leaves.

A small clearing ahead.

He shoved her in front of him.

One step forward.

Pressuring down with his left foot. Leaping into the air.

Twisting, turning, to face their pursuers.

Two of them.

No, three, as another head appeared between the trees.

No others in sight.

The HK leaping into his hands with robotic efficiency.

A long burst streaking out. Hot lead pouring out at 950 rounds per minute.

Speeding out at 730 meters a second.

Death on steroids.

All of them went wide.

But they had the desired effect.

The terrorists slowed. Ducked behind trees.

Zeb landed. Swiveled on his foot.

Joined her. Running fast.

Then they were falling. Rolling on gravel.

A startled scream escaping from her.

His eyes taking everything in. Like a digital camera on rapid speed.

The treeline had given way to a steep bank. No early warning of it.

One moment, dense trees.

The next, a slope of stones and gravel that led to a stream at the bottom.

A range of mountains in the distance. Snow on a couple of peaks.

Standing tall. Proud. Arrogant. Uncaring about what happened to mere mortals.

Zeb dug in his heels. Slowed his descent.

'Ma'am,' he hissed.

Her strained face turned to him.

'Trees. Go to the trees.'

The forest curved around the bank. To their left was the treeline.

A hundred feet away.

No shooters in sight at the top.

They would come, however.

And he would be ready.

She didn't argue. She didn't question. She got to her feet, stumbling.

And took off towards the sanctuary of the wilderness.

He marveled at her ready acceptance of his directives.

And then remembered she was an Iraqi Yazidi.

She's probably seen more death than I have. She knows when to escape.

Then two heads appeared at the top. Rashly.

Not expecting him to be there.

He forgot about her.

His HK chattered. One man fell. The other tried to get back.

Lost his balance.

Rolled down.

Directly toward Zeb.

Chapter 24

Zeb watched the killer tumble, his hands seeking purchase, trying to slow his descent.

One of his hands got hold of his HK. Started bringing around its barrel.

And Zeb was on him. Punching him. Batting away his weapon.

Knuckles shaped like an arrowhead, bursting the terrorist's larynx. Hauling him up when the third man appeared at the top.

Using Namir's man as cover.

Unleashing his weapon and firing from his hip.

Making the man duck and disappear from sight.

Zeb dropped the dead man, and, in a couple of seconds, relieved him of his weapon and the rest of his belongings.

No such thing as too many HKs or water canteens.

He counted the seconds in his mind. Threw one last glance to the top.

No hostile presence.

Sped toward the trees.

He ran hard, swerving around bushes, branches slapping his face, until from somewhere before him, a low call sounded.

'I am here.'

Chapter 25

Sara Ashland came from behind a fir.

Her taut eyes flicked over him. She turned to start running, but he stopped her.

'Wait.'

We ran for maybe a mile. The bank is behind us. We're running parallel to it.

'That way,' he pointed in a direction away from the bank.

'That'll take us towards them,' she objected, even as she broke into a lope.

'Behind them,' he corrected.

'You can carry all those?' She asked over her shoulder, referring to the killers' belongings.

He didn't answer. Followed close behind her, occasionally looking back.

There were no signs of pursuit. He didn't think there would be.

Namir will take stock. He has lost three men. He will take some time to strategize.

In his mind, he pictured a map of the wilderness.

They were between the Middle Fork Salmon and the mountain range.

They were heading into a trail-less area.

Firs and pine extended as far as the eye could see.

If this is new country for me, it's even more so for Namir. He will not follow blindly.

He could hear the girl panting ahead, but she didn't slow down.

Left, then right, straight ahead occasionally, running where the ground was harder, where no tracks could be left.

He brought them to a halt after ninety minutes of bursts of running.

She leaned against a tree and slid down as if her legs had turned to jelly.

She drank greedily from a canteen he thrust at her, drops trickling down her chin and falling to the ground.

She returned it with a whispered thanks and closed her eyes, her chest heaving.

'Why did we stop?'

'We were making too much noise.'

'Won't they catch up?'

'No. They won't resume the hunt for a while.'

'How do you know?'

Because I would have done just that.

'What's your story?' he asked instead.

Her eyes flew open. 'You mean, how did a Yazidi end up in America? With her father dead?'

Bitterness in her voice. The previous night returning to her, now that the adrenaline of flight was wearing out.

'You first,' she challenged him. 'I need to know who I am with. No hiker I know does that.'

Her hand waved in the direction of the bank.

'Are you a killer and rapist? Like them?'

He kept his face expressionless even though his insides tightened.

'What do you think, ma'am?'

'I stopped thinking since I watched my father die, Mr. Carter. Just last night.'

'Right now, I am just *being*.'

Chapter 26

He considered his response, knowing she was watching him closely.

I'm a Special Forces operative. I work in an outfit called The Agency. Nope, that will sound far-fetched, even though it's true.

'I am an FBI agent, ma'am. SWAT. I am on vacation.'

Wind blew through the forest, making the trees sigh and creak. Sunlight pierced through the thick canopy overhead and made irregular patterns on the ground.

'I believe you,' she said after a long while.

'Just like that? Why? I could be lying to you.'

'I know you killed someone in the night. When you said we needed a gun. I heard the shots. And then today, I saw what you did on the gravel.'

'So?'

'I woke sometime in the morning. After you had put me under that tree trunk. I was watching you for some time. You are a killer, Mr. Carter.'

'Zeb. You know a lot of killers, ma'am?'

'Please drop that ma'am nonsense. That's another reason why I believe you. Some FBI people came to visit our home a while back. They were older than you. I was maybe ten or eleven. All of them *ma'am-ed* me. Ma'am this. Ma'am that.

'You forget where I came from, Zeb,' she said, returning to his question. 'I have known killers all my life.'

'I was just a little girl when I saw an ISIS man behead a group of Yazidis.'

He removed a couple of power bars from the dead man's pack and offered one to her.

Her face was all hard planes and angles, the muscles in her cheeks and neck working as she bit and swallowed.

'You are different, however. You are not like any of the terrorists I have seen.'

He waited for her to explain, but she didn't. She carried on as if there wasn't anything more to be discussed about him.

'I am from Mosul,' she carried on. 'I didn't know who my folks were. Our pir, priest, took me in. I lived with several families. We fled to the Sinjar Mountains when the ISIS atrocities increased.'

Another bite. A drink of water.

'There, Dad found me. He was reporting for the New York Times.' Her face softened. 'I don't know what he saw in me. He was alone. Had no one. I was the same. We bonded so well, it was like he *was* my father.'

'He brought me to the U.S. when I was ten years old. I started a new life. I don't know who he bribed, or how much, but I got my citizenship three years ago. He used to call me his princess. Because I changed his life. He certainly changed mine.'

Her voice broke off into a sob.

She finished the bar and emptied the canteen, her eyes unfocused, her lips trembling.

'How old are you?'

'Fifteen.'

'You sound like an adult.'

'I have lived an adult life. I have seen more of life than most grown people do.'

He thought about her timeline. 'You came to the States the same year he reported on Namir?'

'Yes. He brought me over here, first. Then he went to Beirut, where he came across Namir in that church. He was still with the Times then. Once the story exploded, he got all kinds of awards. A Presidential medal. We moved to Erilyn. He wanted a life for us away from the spotlight.'

'Why Erilyn?'

'His hometown. His father was alive. Is alive. He wanted to live close to him. We had a good life. And now …'

'You get along with your grandfather?'

The teenager in her surfaced. She could barely control an eyeroll. 'Gramps? I love him. He lives three blocks away from us.'

'Then, I will take you to him.'

'You are forgetting something,' she snarled, her anger returning. 'Namir and his men. I am a witness. They won't rest until they kill me. And you.'

He shrugged. 'I am forgetting nothing.'

'We will go through them.'

Chapter 27

Zeb pictured a map of the region in his mind as they walked.

A hundred and twenty miles from the mountains. Erilyn is to our northeast, hundred and thirty miles away. The Middle Fork Salmon River is in between.

My camp's to our south. Stanley's closer. Some other towns, too. But they are small. No police presence.

They would have to cross the Middle Fork Salmon River. Several creeks. Rugged terrain. Forests and some open flats. Not many trails.

He had dropped his sat phone at the tree trunks. Lost Abbas's phone, too, when fleeing from the bank. They had one water canteen and a few power bars between them.

He took stock of his weapons: his Glocks and several mags for them, the two HKs and fifteen mags.

Just that, with twenty terrorists hunting them.

Twenty-one originally, including Namir, he corrected himself. *Now eighteen.*

That reminded him. He dug into his pocket and brought out the wallet of the man he had killed on the bank.

Emin Khider. The name leaped out at him from the identity

card. The card had an organization name on it and an address. A Saudi Arabian business, from the looks of it.

He stopped and frowned.

Abbas had some currency in his, but nothing to identify him. Khider ... Why does Namir have Saudis in his group?

'Did Namir say anything? Why he had come? His plans?'

She leaned against a tree and wiped sweat away from her face. 'No. Just that he had waited a long time. To kill Dad. Why?'

He showed her the identity card.

'He's Saudi?' she asked in surprise.

'Yeah,' he said grimly. 'It's a fake. That other man, yesterday night. They called him Abbas.'

'They came as businessmen?'

'Yeah. But I don't think they came for your father alone,' he replied, grimly. 'That many men. It would be a risk. Namir is planning something else.'

'We have to tell someone,' she stood upright, worry and urgency in her face.

'No phones ... wait.' He patted his pocket and brought out a black cellphone. 'This belonged to Khider.'

'Use it.'

'No. I now know how they found us at those tree trunks. Why my sat phone didn't work.'

'How?'

'Namir's tracking all these phones. He tracked Abbas's cell. He's using jammers, too. Sophisticated devices that can shut down a sat phone, too.'

'In the entire forest?'

'No. They have a radius. The good ones, military-grade, the kind the FBI uses ... those have a range of one hundred and fifty meters.'

'You should turn off that cell,' she said, moistening her lips nervously.

He looked at the device in his hand, a plan forming in his mind.

'No. We'll leave it on.'

'They'll find us.'

'That's the plan.'

They made contact with the enemy just before ten am on Wednesday.

Chapter 28

Zeb was following Sara Ashland when he smelled a whiff of smoke.

He tugged her hoodie and made her stop, holding a finger to his lips.

He sniffed. Yes, no doubt. Cigarette smoke.

He saw her breathe deeply too, recognition dawning in her eyes when she placed the odor.

'It could be campers,' she whispered.

Hikers had been on his mind. He had deliberately chosen his camp to be far from any travelers. However, the wilderness had many visitors. They were bound to encounter a few.

Namir will kill them.

He motioned her to the ground and tried to get a wind direction.

The smell came from their left.

He pulled out Khider's phone. Removed its battery and SIM card, and crushed the device.

They started crawling slowly, him taking the lead.

Barely fifty yards had passed when bushes rustled ahead.

He held up a hand to stop her and pointed with his index finger to a thicket.

Turned his head around to watch her insert herself carefully in the bushes.

He resumed moving, faster, now that he didn't have to worry about her.

Got to his feet when he was out of her vision.

Used trees to shield himself.

Two men came from behind a dense bunch of pines, their eyes on something one terrorist held.

No time to think.

He was moving even before his brain had processed what his eyes saw.

They were close, almost shoulder to shoulder, their HKs dangling from their shoulders.

Their eyes lifted when they sensed him.

Zeb flew at them, his HK swinging around in a wicked arc.

Its barrel crashed into the first killer's neck. He dropped the tracker to the ground, a cry bursting out of his lips.

Zeb kneed him, and smashed his rifle's barrel on the back of his neck.

The second killer was reacting.

Swiftly.

His mouth opening to warn the rest of Namir's men. His body taking several steps back to give himself room.

His HK swinging around. Turning to aim at Zeb.

Zeb threw away his weapon and pounced at him.

His left forearm came up, beneath the hostile's gun.

Deflected its barrel just as rounds burst from it and sprayed the branches above them.

His fingers jabbed at the shooter's eyes. A scream that

escaped Namir's man died away in a choking gasp when Zeb's elbow crushed his neck.

The beast roared to life suddenly, flew through Zeb's fingers and rammed the killer against the nearest tree.

Zeb smashed the man's head against the trunk.

Once. Twice. Until his body sagged.

Zeb let him go and stood back, breathing lightly.

Five down.

Chapter 29

Sara Ashland's face turned white and a shiver passed through her when he returned and threw the shooter's weapons under a bush.

'Two men? They are …'

'They won't trouble us anymore.'

She blinked rapidly and jammed her hands deep in her pockets—but not before he noticed them trembling.

He didn't comment. He knew what she was going through. He had experienced it himself and seen it in many victims.

Shock came first, when a parent or a close relative was killed in a brutal manner.

Then came grief.

Rage and anger came last.

In her case, she's had no time to go through all those emotions. And now she's with me. She isn't sure if we will see another sunrise.

He toyed with the tracker he had taken off the two men.

'Is that what I think it is?'

'Yeah. See,' he turned the screen to her and tapped buttons. 'That green dot. That was Abbas's phone. They must have been wondering why it went offline suddenly. That's why they didn't notice me.'

She looked nervously behind her. 'There are many more, still. They could be close.'

'They are nearby, but not that close. I think I know how they are working.'

He squatted and reached out for a stick.

He cleared the ground of leaves and drew a rough map of the wilderness.

'This was where my camp was.' He jabbed at the ground.

'This is where I reckon you were.' He made a cross to the east of his camp.

She nodded. 'I guess so. Your map-drawing skills … you don't have any.'

He jerked his head up to see a small smile appear on her lips and disappear just as fast.

'This was the bank.' He drew a curved line. 'We ran here, and now we are here.'

'I thought we had left them behind. But Namir's turning out to be smarter than I thought,' he acknowledged. 'He and his men followed in our direction. In the dense forest, he got them strung out. Maybe groups of two or three, about 200 meters apart. Each group carrying a tracker. Following Abbas's phone.'

'Why 200 meters?'

He produced the cellphone jammer the second killer had been carrying.

'Because of this baby. It blocks phone signals. This one has a range of 200 meters. This is hard-to-find gear. Only American and British Special Forces use these. Mossad as well. Namir's groups are carrying one of these, too. To block any calls I make or receive.

'You don't have your phone, though.'

'They are assuming I might have another. Good thinking on their part.'

Her body grew tense, her hands twitched, her voice dropped to a whisper.

'If they are just 200 meters away, they could be coming. They would have heard the shooting.'

'Yes. I want them to come.'

Chapter 30

She looked at him like he was crazy, but dropped to the ground when he began crawling.

She hissed in anger and fear when he started heading in the direction from which the dead gunmen had come.

'That's where they are. That line of men you drew.'

'Yeah,' he whispered. 'They'll be expecting us to run.'

'There are still sixteen of them.'

'No.' He raised a hand to silence her. Explanations could come later.

Namir won't send all sixteen at once. He doesn't even know if I am alone. He'll deploy one or two groups. Four or six men.

He counted time and distance in his mind.

Ten minutes since the fight.

Normal walking speed of adults, five kilometers an hour. Eight hundred meters in ten minutes.

But these conditions are different. They'll first call their killers. See if they are alive.

Then track their phones. Khider's, too. They will move cautiously, stop every now and then.

They'll discuss among themselves. Namir will give them orders.

So, twenty or thirty minutes to get to the dead men.

He started seeking cover after ten minutes.

Anything dense and thick, at ground level.

There were ponderosas ahead. Thick trunks, large enough to shield both of them. Gnarly branches that snaked out, blocking the sun.

He stopped.

Why hide in the bushes?

She bumped into him from behind and looked at him angrily.

Move, she mouthed.

He raised his hand and pointed to the branches.

Can you climb?

Another eyeroll was his answer.

She didn't need any help.

She grabbed a branch, powered herself up nimbly, and went up high in the tree, lost from his sight.

He went ahead ten meters. Stopped just after a small rise, next to another giant trunk, with bushes and knee-high growth to hide him.

There was no hard cover to protect him, but that wasn't the point.

He prayed she couldn't see him. Wouldn't watch what would happen next.

Because there was no mercy in him.

His pulse slowed as he waited. Sound amplified.

He stretched out and brought the HK to his shoulder.

No ghillie suit for camouflage. However, his jacket was olive-colored, his jeans brown. They would blend in.

He sighted the rifle and waited.

Somewhere high above, a bird screeched. An animal grunted.

Black bear?

And then, a footfall sounded. Soft. Careful.

From the direction he had guessed.

He didn't celebrate when a head peered from around a tree.

This wasn't party time. It was killing time.

Chapter 31

The man was twenty feet away. His bearded head didn't move much. His eyes scanned the ground carefully.

They skipped over Zeb's hide and roamed beyond and behind.

He seemed to make some kind of hand signal, and then clothing rustled and another man joined him.

Their lips moved. One of them raised a cell to his mouth and spoke softly, too far away for Zeb to overhear.

They spread out, making their way carefully, their guns ahead of them. One man holding his tracker in his left hand.

Not using the jammer. Because they need to stay in touch.

Zeb could hear them breathing as they passed on his right. He could have taken them out.

There's one more team, however. At least.

The second team appeared when the first was nearly out of sight.

Two more men, both bearded, farther away from him, to his right again.

They were keeping an eye on both the first team and the terrain ahead of them.

He waited.

Time was on his side.

The battleground was of his choosing.

He was confident they wouldn't find the girl. No one would.

Not even me. Climbing a tree wouldn't occur to anyone.

The men at the rear came closer, and then started veering off, to keep that angle between them and the first team.

They paused for a moment, conferring with each other. Their chests presenting to him.

Zeb took the shot.

A short burst, left to right, from waist-high to head.

A second burst, right to left, from head to waist.

He was moving even before the men had fallen.

Bending low. Running toward them. Firing another burst when he passed them. And then he was diving, as the first team reacted.

He rolled as the first burst of fire sprayed behind him.

His HK came up, long bursts firing in the direction of the attackers.

Moving continually, slithering and sliding, keeping them pinned down.

Fast mag change. A desperate roll as a round gouged the earth in front of him and sprayed dirt in his eyes.

Finish this quickly.

He reached a tree trunk, sheltered behind it, and went through his options.

A shout from deeper inside the forest reminded him more men would come soon.

He snapped a glance around the bole.

Both men hurrying in his direction.

Spread out. Twenty feet away.

Wood chipped from the trunk when one of them fired in his direction.

He was planning to dive to the ground and fire in one roll. It could be suicidal, but it was the only alternative.

'I am here.'

Chapter 32

Sara Ashland called from behind the first team.

Zeb flashed a quick look.

The team stopped. One man flicked a glance back. The second turned his head at an angle.

That was the only distraction Zeb needed.

'Down!' he roared at the girl, and his HK chattered.

He unslung the second one with his left hand, and triggered it, too.

Twin streams of lead, racing through the forest, thudding into flesh and wood, extracting screams from the men and ripping out branches and leaves.

He ran out, ducked over their fallen bodies and grabbed spare magazines from them.

Fired into the body of one man who was still alive.

Grabbed the girl's hand as she rose from behind a tree.

And fled.

Northeast. In the direction of Erilyn. Away from the dead men.

He heard shouts in the distance: the rest of the terrorists. The sounds grew distant and then faded as he urged the girl to go faster, while looking back occasionally to check for pursuers.

They ran hard for half an hour, after which she started flagging.

He started looking for shelter, something that would hide them, where they could rest.

They passed an abandoned hut someone had constructed in a small clearing.

Saw her questioning look but ignored it.

No huts. That will be the first place they look.

They slowed to a walk. And then he saw it, a few seconds before she did.

They were on a downward slope, firs and pines extending down the hill ahead of them.

But at some point there had been a landslide at this spot, and boulders, some of them chest-high, had rolled down to where a grove of trees stopped them at the bottom.

The rocks, with rotting trees piled up against them, formed a natural alcove.

He reloaded his HKs automatically, his eyes sectoring the possible hide.

It looked good.

He approached it cautiously and spotted a small opening between two rocks. He had to crouch to go through it and then crawl beneath a trunk, but once inside, the space became wider and higher. A natural cave. Not fully enclosed, but good enough to shelter the girl.

She followed him inside, a tight squeeze.

'Will we spend the night here?'

'No. Just a few hours.'

'Why?'

'Food. We need something to eat.'

'Hunting? I'll come with you.'

He thought of arguing but didn't. *She'll be safer with me.*

He rolled beneath the rotting trunk and crawled outside again.

His jacket caught on the boulder's rough surface, his rifles clanking. He freed his outerwear and was rising, then froze.

An HK was pointed straight at him.

Two inches away from his neck.

Chapter 33

Sara Ashland gasped when her eyes fell on the terrorist.

He was grinning through his beard, his eyes dancing.

'I got you.' Thickly accented English.

He started reaching into his jacket with his free hand.

Zeb made his move.

One hand shoved the girl away, to safety.

His other hand flew up, its palm jerking the barrel towards the sky.

The killer fired reflexively, the bullet burning a hot furrow into Zeb's jacket as it grazed his left shoulder.

Zeb ignored it.

He body-slammed the shooter, crushing him against the boulder.

A hoarse shout escaped Namir's man.

He struggled, punched, kicked, and tried to get control over his HK.

Zeb ignored the blows. Compartmentalized the fiery lance that shot through him when a flailing hand jabbed his wound.

He caught the man's chin.

And smashed his head back against the rock.

The assailant's thick, shaggy hair absorbed most of the blow.

Zeb headbutted him, just as the killer's knee rose, seeking his groin.

He twisted. Took the blow on his thigh, and headbutted the terrorist again.

His forehead broke his attacker's nose.

The man howled and punched Zeb in the throat.

Zeb's vision went dark momentarily, but he counterattacked.

He caught hold of the terrorist's rifle barrel and yanked, catching the killer caught off-guard.

As he stumbled forward, Zeb punched him in the mouth with a bent elbow.

The man's howl became a scream.

His lips split. His teeth broke.

His cries turned feeble when Zeb crushed his head repeatedly against the rock.

Then they stopped.

Zeb looked around for a fraction of a second.

Sara Ashland was still on the ground, shaking her head in a daze.

No other terrorist came crashing through the forest. No alarmed or angry yells sounded.

He picked up the shooter and heaved him across his shoulder.

'Get back inside,' he told the girl. 'Use the HK if you have to.'

He carried the dead gunman back the way he had come. Deep into the cover of the trees.

A wide, meandering circle, all the while looking out for other hostiles.

RUN!

He dumped the body in a clearing half a mile away from the rocks.

He took the man's cell, sprinted another half-mile, and fired several times into the sky.

Ten men down.

Namir will track his phone and hear the shots. They will assume the dead man is on our trail.

A diversionary tactic.

Enough to buy us time.

I hope, he thought.

Chapter 34

Zeb was pleased when he saw no sign of the girl on his return.

There were no signs of a struggle. No traces of blood on the rock.

She's erased the tracks. Cleaned up the boulder.

'It's me,' he called out softly. He heard her rustling inside.

Her eyes were wide, her lips thinned, when he entered and rested against a rotting trunk.

'You moved so fast,' she said wonderingly.

'I was careless,' he replied bitterly. 'I should have been alert.'

'Where did he come from?' She placed the HK on the ground and drank a swig from the canteen they shared.

'A scout.' Zeb closed his eyes and willed his control to return. 'Namir must have sent him out in advance. That dude must have cast a wide loop. He probably heard us. He was too close to me. That was his mistake. Besides, he was reaching for his phone as well. And that was his death.'

'You are hit,' she breathed.

Her words reminded him. He looked down at his left shoulder.

His jacket was ripped. His T-shirt, too.

Both were dark and bloodied.

He could feel a growing patch of damp on his upper chest.

He probed lightly with his fingers and breathed an inward sigh of relief when he saw the wound.

'The round scraped some flesh away. Less than a quarter of an inch. No great damage.'

He removed his outer clothing and took the canteen from her.

He wet his T-shirt with water and cleaned the wound. Tore a strip off the shirt and got the girl to bind it tight.

Donned what was left of his shirt and put on his jacket again.

Rotated his arm experimentally.

It hurt. But it moved freely.

Better than being dead.

'We need to move. Namir might have sent more scouts.'

'What were those shots I heard?'

The slope leveled off in front of their hide and became a large plain. It didn't have much cover. Just knee-high rolling grass and bushes. The tree line started a mile away.

'We need to clear that,' he said, ignoring her question. 'Fast. You good to run?'

'You promised food,' she whined, the way millions of teenagers did.

'Once we are out of the open.'

She took off without a word, arms and legs pumping.

'Not in a straight line,' he called out.

She shot him a look, but started zigging and zagging.

Fifteen minutes later, they were sheltered by the forest, but she kept going.

He caught her by her hoodie to slow her down and shushed her when she swung back.

'Smoke,' he whispered, breathing deeply.

'There's someone else here.'

Chapter 35

Namir kicked his scout's body savagely.

He and the rest of his men had arrived at the site forty-five minutes after they tracked his phone. They had discovered the other bodies, too. Scattered in the forest. A couple of them bent and broken. Most of them shot.

His plan had worked. To an extent. Stringing his men out with jammers and trackers had brought them into contact with the stranger.

But the result angered him.

'Who is this man?' he roared into the forest.

Not one of his men dared to reply.

He paced as his men grouped loosely around him, some of them looking down at their trackers.

The sight angered him.

'That didn't help,' he said, grabbing one device, flinging it to the ground, and stomping on it.

'Sayidi, he is just one man,' Osman, one of his killers, said softly.

'*Not Arabic. Only English*,' Namir screamed, showering the man in spittle.

'And how do you know he is just one man? That girl might not even be with him.'

He snatched a water canteen from one of his men and drank deeply. He wiped his mouth on his sleeve. 'We need to think like him,' he said, calmer. 'This man is a fox. We need to be a wolf.'

'He will go to Erilyn,' he said, after several moments of thinking. 'That's the largest town near this godforsaken place. It has police. Her grandfather—he lives there.' He snapped his fingers, remembering the background research on Kenton Ashland.

'You know the route Khalid took?' He glared at Osman.

Khalid was the dead scout.

'Yes, sayidi ... yes,' his man stammered. 'It is on his tracker.'

'We will backtrack that route. His last movement. This man is cunning. It is possible he killed Khalid somewhere else and dumped his body here. The place of the kill—it is from there he and the girl will go to Erilyn.'

'*Move!*' he yelled at his men when they remained motionless.

They scrambled to attention and started filing in the direction Osman pointed.

Namir brought up the rear, glowering. He didn't bother to hide Khalid's body. None of his dead killers were buried.

That's what they get. For being killed by one man.

Doubts began to rise in him, however. *Can one man kill ten of my men? My people are killers. Trained as terrorists. They are not ordinary men. Only someone exceptional could kill them.*

The hut had held only one person's possessions, however.

One sleeping bag. The stranger's computers had erased themselves when he had tried to use them. His sat phone had done the same.

No, it's just one man. And the girl is with him. We found her hair.

He's a soldier. On vacation. Some special unit. No one else will have that kind of equipment, he thought, recollecting the spare batteries, the wicked-looking blade, and the armored vest left behind in the hut.

It didn't matter. The man's luck would not last.

He still had ten cold-blooded murderers, some of the most wanted men, with him.

They would find their targets.

And then I will rape her in front of him. Let my men have their fun, too.

Only then will I kill him.

Slowly.

Chapter 36

The smoke seemed to be right ahead of them.

Zeb peered between the trees. No wisps arising from anywhere.

He motioned for Sara Ashland to stay close as he moved quietly.

There came a splash and the sound of someone whistling. He cocked his head.

Running water? A stream?

It felt like flowing water.

They were on a downward slope again. A gradual decline.

There could be water flowing at the bottom.

Would Namir's men whistle, however? Would they be so careless?

There was a stream. A very small one, two feet wide. More like a rivulet.

Zeb watched in amazement from beneath a large bush at the bottom of the slope.

A white, bearded man in a sleeveless T-shirt and jeans was standing outside a tent. Dirty sneakers on his feet.

His camp was in a small clearing on the other side of the

flowing water.

Around his waist was a gunbelt. Zeb thought his handgun was a Sig Sauer.

Something was cooking on a portable stove. Giving off wisps of smoke.

'Who is he?' the girl whispered.

I don't know every person on the planet. Zeb bit back his retort.

One pm on Wednesday.

The absence of campers had bothered him.

Now, he seemed to be looking at the first hiker.

Stay back, he mouthed at the girl, and stood up.

He stepped out carefully toward the stranger.

The man didn't notice him until he was out of the woods and approaching the small clearing.

'Huh?' the man gawped when he noticed Zeb.

His eyes went wide when they took in the HKs.

His hand blurred towards his Sig.

'*No!*' Zeb dove at him and brought him to the ground.

Clamped a wrist around his gun hand.

The stranger twisted and punched him in the face.

Zeb's head rang, but he didn't let up. He absorbed all the blows, a few falling on his wounded shoulder and sending fire racing through him.

He kept on squeezing, however, until the man groaned and let go of his weapon.

Zeb applied an armlock and twisted the man's shoulder.

The stranger tried to kick back.

'Don't,' Zeb warned him.

The man reared back and stunned him with a sharp elbow. Then, Zeb dislocated the man's shoulder.

He got up and dusted his hands as the man shrieked in agony.

He tested his jaw. No damage. But it hurt.

His shoulder was bleeding again, but it would heal. More importantly, the wound didn't restrict his movement.

The stranger cursed, got up gingerly—and made a run at Zeb.

Who slapped him and knocked him to the ground.

'Who are you?' Zeb kneeled over him.

'Who the f—'

Zeb slapped him. 'Language.'

'Who are you?' the man asked, sullenly.

'I asked first.'

The stranger looked at him, and then at Sara Ashland, who came out of the forest.

'You're in trouble,' he said, his lips parting in a wicked smirk. 'You just walked into a big heap of it.'

'Trouble? What kind?'

The man started to gesture with his hand and broke off in a grimace. 'Behind me,' he jerked his head, 'Are several acres of pot. I guard it.

'Dude, you just stumbled onto the Tavez Cartel's farm.'

Chapter 37

Sara Ashland's face turned ashen.

The Tavez Cartel was one of the most vicious drug gangs in the world—Mexico-based, but with a growing network in the U.S.

It wasn't as large as the Cali Cartel or the Sinaloa gang, but it was fast acquiring a reputation as the most vicious.

Joachim Tavez wanted to take over territory. He was more than happy to wage war with other gangs.

There was a video of him on the Internet, executing shooters from the Cali Cartel after first torturing them.

'This is too far for that gang,' Zeb said, scorning the stranger.

'That's exactly why Tavez has this farm. Right here. No one will suspect it,' the stranger cackled.

Zeb knew illegal pot farms were a growing menace in the forests of the country.

The areas involved were remote, usually uninhabited but for visitors.

Their inaccessibility played right into the hands of drug gangs.

'Why should I believe you?'

'Don't, buddy. Hang around for a few hours. A bunch of cartel shooters will arrive. Accompanied by the boss man himself. He takes a personal interest. Which you'd know if you have heard of him. He will come with laborers. To harvest the farm and carry it away. Just stick around. You will see.'

'If I were you,' he snarled, 'I would run. Get away and never speak about this. Otherwise, you and your lady—you might get some unwelcome guests.'

He had risen while speaking and taken a couple of steps toward his tent.

Suddenly, he dived toward it, his uninjured arm reaching inside.

It came out with a Mossberg shotgun.

Its barrel started swinging. Turning in the visitors' direction.

Zeb waited until the last split-second, then leaned forward and grasped the barrel. Twisted it up and slammed the shotgun back against the stranger.

Its stock caught him flush on the chin. The angry crack of the blow was drowned by his scream.

The stranger fell back, clutching his jaw, all fight leaving him.

'We should go,' the girl said, putting a tentative hand on Zeb's shoulder.

He read her fear.

First Namir killed her father. Now this, a deadly cartel.

'We will,' he assured her. 'But not until we get some supplies.'

'What supplies?' the guard moaned.

'Food. Water. We are taking your stock. You have a cellphone?'

The man gaped at Zeb, tried to laugh, and winced.

'Cellphone? There's no coverage here. Not for miles.'

'Where's your phone?'

He dug it out and threw it at Zeb. 'See for yourself.'

No bars. He's right.

'Listen carefully,' Zeb told him sternly. 'There is a bunch of terrorists in the wilderness. Hunting us. Get out of here. Go to the cops. Tell them. Warn any hikers you see. These guys are bearded. Carry HKs. They can't be mistaken.'

The cartel man chuckled. 'Some story. You expect me to believe that? You're just a pair of thieves.'

Sara Ashland sprang forward and slapped him. Hard.

His head snapped to the left. A dull flush spread over his face. He reached out to grab her and fell back when she kicked him in the belly.

'Those terrorists tortured my father. Killed him in front of me. Yesterday night. You'd better believe that. Because they will do the same to you, if they find you.'

The guard was lost for words for several moments. His mouth opened and closed like a fish's, while he nursed his shoulder.

'I don't care,' he blustered. 'My job is to protect this pot farm. Joachim takes a direct interest in it. Besides, no terrorist is going to mess with the Tavez Cartel.'

'And, I ain't going near any cops,' he squared his shoulders defiantly. 'Or anyone else. Wait. What are you doing?'

Zeb didn't answer. He turned the man around roughly and pulled out his wallet. He rifled through it rapidly until he found a driving license.

'Scot Koeman.' The picture matched the man in front of him.

He tossed the wallet back and went inside the tent.

He came out with a backpack stuffed with food and water canteens. Coffee, mugs, a pan. Matches. A long length of climbing rope.

A piece of rubber hose and several strings went into the bag's pocket. Because one never knew when those would be needed.

Koeman's hunting knives, two of them, were strapped to his thigh.

Sara Ashland grabbed the bag from him while he destroyed the Mossberg and Koeman's Sig.

'You're leaving me unarmed,' the guard cried out in protest.

'The Tavez Cartel—surely they'll protect you.'

Koeman turned mean.

'You had better run hard. Because they protect their own. They will come after you. And it won't be a friendly visit.'

Chapter 38

'You believe him?' Sara Ashland mumbled around a mouthful of sandwich.

'About the cartel growing that pot?'

'Yeah.'

They had left Koeman's camp cautiously and then had watched him from a distance.

The guard made no attempt to follow them. He stomped around in anger, yelled at the sky, but stayed put.

'Yeah,' Zeb replied as he maintained a fast pace. 'I found a ledger in his backpack.'

She looked over his shoulder as he flicked through pages. 'Those are records of pot harvested. Taken away. See those notes at the bottom.'

She sucked in her breath sharply when she made out Koeman's handwriting and read aloud. '"Joachim is not happy. Says there should be more pot. Will cut off my hand if he finds I am cheating."'

'Does the cartel head get involved in something like this?'

'Yes. This one does. He is a micro-manager.'

She looked up with a stricken face. 'He said they will

come after us.'

'For taking Koeman's food and water? No, they won't.'

He looked in her eyes and hoped she believed him.

The cartel will come after us. Because Tavez has a reputation for not letting go of any slight or insult to him or his gang.

His face turned bleak when she upped her pace and overtook him.

Bad enough that we have to deal with a terrorist. Now there's a cartel involved.

They covered twenty miles, Zeb pushing them hard, resting for only short breaks of five minutes.

Detouring past open flats. Going through wild, beautiful country that he would have taken time to enjoy. If he was alone. And no terrorists were behind them.

'They are well behind us,' the girl panted during one fast trot.

'No. We lost some time at Koeman's. Namir will not let up now. Besides, we need to put distance between us and the cartel.'

'You said they wouldn't hunt us.'

'That doesn't mean we should linger around.'

The sooner I can get to Erilyn, the quicker I can hand her over to the cops. And come back, to hunt Namir. And Tavez, if he shows up.

His plan was to cover as many miles as possible that day. Sleep that night. Travel the remaining distance the next couple of days and reach Erilyn either on Saturday evening or early on Sunday.

His plan hit a setback.

It was four pm.

Sara Ashland was doubled up. Her chest heaving. Sweat pouring down her face.

Zeb had opened a canteen and was offering it to her, when the four men came from behind them.

All wearing baseball caps. Two bearded. Two clean-shaven. Of North American or European descent.

All armed, carrying AR-15s or some Chinese rip-off.

'Evening,' said a burly man, who tipped his cap. And stumbled.

'Chuck's had too much to drink,' said the clean-shaven man who caught him before he fell.

Chuck shook him off. 'I am fine. I want to talk to the lady.'

'Not now, Chuck. Let's go,' Clean Shaven urged him, the other two men making similar noises.

'Dammit, Jake. I told ya, I want to talk to her,' the drunk yelled.

He lurched forward.

Zeb stopped him with a palm to his chest.

Chuck growled and raised his AR-15.

Chapter 39

Zeb had had enough of amateurs.

He twisted Chuck's rifle away easily. Tripped him and shoved him onto his ass.

The burly man's face reddened. He scrambled to his feet with an oath and charged at Zeb.

Who punched him in the gut, rolled him across his hip and sent him sprawling—a move from judo, a martial art that uses an opponent's energy and speed against him.

'Don't,' Zeb warned Chuck, one of his HKs coming up to cover all of them, in a seemingly casual manner.

'Jesus. Who the f—' Jake began, moving forward. He stopped when the HK moved an inch.

He friends backed down, too, keeping their hands well away from their weapons.

'I'll ask the questions. Who are you?' Zeb was ready for anything. His ears listening to sounds beyond.

Doesn't look like they are connected to Namir. Or Tavez. But I need to be sure.

'Jesus,' Jake repeated. 'We're campers. You didn't have to hit Chuck so hard. He's bleeding.'

'You got any IDs?'

'Who are you, man? Are you a cop?'

'I am the one holding the gun on you.'

The hikers took one look at Zeb and swallowed their protests. They tossed their driver's licenses at Zeb, who signaled to the girl to pick them up.

'Chuck. Jake. Paul Bo—' she squinted her eyes, reading their first names.

'Bowdrie, ma'am,' a lean man spoke up.

'All from Texas. From Houston.'

'Why are you here?'

'I told you. Camping. We come each year,' Jake replied, impatiently, darting glances at the burly man on the ground. 'Look, man. Ma'am. Chuck was out of line. I apologize for that. But there was no reason to react like that.'

'He was reaching for his gun.'

'He's drunk. I could have reasoned with him. But, no. You had to go Rambo on him. Why are you carrying that many guns, anyway?'

'There are terrorists in the forest,' Sara Ashland cut him short. 'They killed my father. They are hunting us.'

Her words sucked the wind out of them.

She explained briefly as their eyes bugged out.

'How can we help?' Jake scratched his head. 'Our cellphones don't work. We were planning to return tomorrow.'

'Stay together,' Zeb warned them. 'Keep away from any noise you hear. Warn other hikers. Don't play hero. Go back to the nearest town. Report to the cops.'

'You think they'll do that?' the girl asked him, when they were on the move again.

They had taken more water and food supplies from the

campers and left quickly, Zeb conscious of the time they were wasting.

'No.'

'No?' she pivoted on a heel in surprise, nearly falling.

'Yeah. Our story. It is so incredible that no one will believe it. They will talk among themselves. It takes just one person to trash it and they will come around to that man's view.'

He pushed her forward gently, resuming their fast lope. They still had to cover his planned distance.

At six pm they stopped for a breather.

Shared fruit that they had taken from the hikers. Finished a bottle of water.

Started again.

They were approaching a rise that was in the open. There was no way to go around it without sacrificing too much time.

The incline seemed mostly gravel and soft mud, after the dense trees petered out.

Zeb wanted to cross it quickly—minimal exposure against the skyline.

The girl sprinted over it and called out that there was more gravel on the other side, a dry stream bed, and then forest.

The sniper's bullet struck Zeb just as he reached the top of the slope.

It tore into his thigh and brought him down.

Chapter 40

Joachim Tavez reached his pot farm early.

He liked to keep his men on their toes, and arriving at the farm before the scheduled time was part of his method.

He had six shooters with him and ten workers.

Four other gunmen were in the forest, forming a perimeter around the pot farm.

They had flown to Canada, evaded the border patrol by walking by night through farmland along the boundary, then driven to the outskirts of the wilderness, trekking through the forest to the farm.

The stealth was just an extra precaution. Tavez was passing as a Mexican businessman and had ten other fake passports he could use.

He arrived to see Koeman hopping mad. The guard was swearing up a storm as he clutched his shoulder.

'What happened?'

Koeman jumped, startled. His face lost its color when he saw the cartel boss and his men, who had crept up on him silently.

Tavez was five feet ten, lean and clean-shaven, with short,

cropped hair. His darkly tanned face and black eyes could split into a warm smile.

But that warmth was a façade. Joachim Tavez was violent, ruthless and emotionless.

His face could turn cold in an instant. He took pleasure in killing.

Koeman had seen the gang boss enjoy watching a snitch's hands be hacked off.

The guard told him what had happened and closed his eyes for an instant, expecting a bullet to the brain.

'You told him this is my farm?'

'I had no choice. He would have killed me. He had a gun to my head,' Koeman quavered.

'And you think I will let you live?'

'I hope you will. I know how he looks. He won't have gone far. We can find him.'

Tavez looked at his man. Koeman had served him well for a long time. He had not once let the cartel boss down.

Koeman was probably not at fault.

However, Tavez hadn't grown his business by being big-hearted. Carelessness deserved to be punished.

Especially when it concerned the pot farm.

This was a new venture for the drug lord. If he could grow pot in this wilderness, in America, right under the noses of law enforcement, he could grow it in other forests.

He could build cook shops in these wild places. His cost of distribution would plummet.

Tavez was a killer, true, but foremost a businessman. And now, a couple of strangers knew about the farm.

No, such carelessness could not go unpunished.

He nodded to one of his shooters, who produced

a silver-plated Colt, Tavez's personal weapon.

He cocked and pointed it at Koeman, who begged and trembled.

He was pulling the trigger, focused on the guard's terror-stricken face and oblivious to movement around him.

'*Stop!*'

Chapter 41

The cartel boss turned slowly, his shooters much faster, whirling around with M16s at the ready to confront the strangers.

Eleven of them, Tavez counted. Well-armed, pointing weapons at him and his men.

'We call this a Mexican standoff,' he grinned, turning on the charm.

The leader, a bearded man with fierce eyes, didn't smile. He sized up the gang boss with an impenetrable expression on his face.

'Who are you?'

'I should ask that question,' Tavez replied. 'You are in my territory. Pointing guns at me.'

'Where did the man and the girl go?'

'You heard? You know them?' the Mexican's gaze sharpened.

'I have business with them.'

'What kind?'

'I have business with *them*. Not you.'

Tavez clenched his teeth. He was outnumbered. This wasn't the place to start a gunfight.

'I have business with them, too.'

'Your men know this forest? We can hunt them together, if they do.'

'Who are you, and why should I trust you? You are not American.'

'Neither are you,' the stranger said, smiling crookedly. 'I know that smell. I know your accent. I can guess what kind of man you are.'

'So can I.'

'They are getting away as we talk. Are you in? Or shall we start shooting?'

Joachim Tavez was the most feared man in Mexico, his name one of the best-known in the world.

Those who knew him knew he wasn't a man to be crossed. And yet, this stranger stood here challenging him, uncaring that he would be one of the first to die if bullets started to fly.

The Mexican felt a grudging respect for the man.

There was the fact, for starters, that the stranger and his ten men had somehow slipped past his security cordon. Someone would die for that.

But for now, the newcomer was right.

The unknown man and the girl were slipping away. But still, there was the matter of trust.

'Who are you?'

'Why does it matter? We could have opened fire on you without warning.'

'You would have died.'

'So would you.'

Tavez didn't believe in hunches. He never trusted people.

He did something he never had in his life.

He signaled his men to lower their weapons.

And that's how his sniper team of Gomes, Hector and Enrico joined Namir, who pushed them hard through the forest, not bothering with concealment or stealth.

Because finding Sara Ashland and whoever was with her was more important.

For both the Lebanese gang and the Mexicans.

Soon they had a stroke of luck, when Enrico noticed a filament hanging off a branch — from the hoodie the girl wore.

That confirmed they were on the right track, and half an hour later, they thought they heard the girl talking.

Then Gomes caught sight of the man and the girl. Gomes, the best cartel sniper in Mexico, who then fell flat on his belly.

Brought his scope to his eye.

Breathed in and out, while Namir halted everyone else.

And Gomes fired the shot, just as the man was crossing the ridge.

Chapter 42

Zeb could feel incoming danger the way animals can sense it.

But before he could react, the round slammed into his left thigh.

He had been fired upon several times in his life. He had experienced more severe injuries than a bullet to his leg.

So now, his training and experience took over.

He allowed his body to fall limply. Weight and gravity took over and dragged him down the slope, beyond the sight line of the sniper.

In the distance he heard the yips of his pursuers.

Namir and his men, he thought. *He knows I am hit. They came quicker than I expected.*

And then he stopped worrying about them.

Because Sara Ashland's face was in front of him. Crying. Grasping at him. Helping him stand.

'Ten minutes,' he said, gritting his teeth.

'What?' she sobbed.

'We have ten minutes before they come. Get to cover. Hide. Take this.' He thrust one of Koeman's knives at her.

He took long hops, ignoring the pain. Ignoring that he even

had a left leg. His body could protest and groan all it wanted.

He would become Zen.

'Dig a hole. Leaves. Branches to cover yourself. Take this.' He cut a section of rubber tube he had found in the guard's tent. 'Use it to breathe. Like you are underwater.'

'Give me a safe word.'

'What?' She was gulping enormous breaths of air. Sucking in oxygen. The sounds of pursuit were coming clearer now.

'Ma'am!'—he grabbed her shoulders, blinking his eyes rapidly to dislodge sweat—'Listen to me. Carefully.'

He repeated his instructions, looking deeply into her eyes. He sighed inwardly with relief when her eyes turned intelligent again, and she nodded in understanding.

'Give me a safe word.'

'Tulip,' she replied promptly, not asking why he wanted one.

'Tulip?'

'Yeah. It's Gramps' cat.'

'Go. Don't think of me. I will deal with them. We will be fine.'

Her strained face bobbed, and she fled.

Zeb waited for the forest to swallow her and then looked back.

Three figures were racing down the slope.

Eight, maybe nine minutes away.

One of them shouted and pointed in his direction.

Zeb hobbled toward the protection offered by the firs.

A shot rang out, the bullet losing itself in the forest, and then he was out of their sight.

He stopped immediately and looked around.

For a moment he thought of digging a hole in the ground and burying himself.

The way he had asked the girl to do.

No time for that. Will require too much effort.

He looked up.

Branches. And leafy cover.

Favoring his right leg, he jumped as high he could.

He slipped and bit back an oath when he landed on his left leg and agony raced through him.

He leaped again.

Hooked his right hand around a branch and pulled himself up.

Got his right leg over the branch, and levered his body through sheer dint of will.

He was ten feet above the ground now. Waiting, Koeman's second hunting knife in his hand. One of his Glocks within easy reach.

At Koeman's tent, he had pocketed several strings that he now used to tie the HKs to his waist to prevent them from clanking.

A simple tug would release them and bring either one to hand for quick use.

He wiped sweat off his eyes and hunkered down.

Someone would die in the next few minutes.

He hoped it wouldn't be him.

Or the girl.

Chapter 43

Zeb moistened his lips. Stopped thinking about Sara Ashland. Only his pursuers mattered.

Namir will not send all. He has lost too many men. Tavez won't, either. He is in a new situation.

Those three men I saw. They'll come.

No more, I hope.

Time didn't matter anymore. He worked out various scenarios in his mind for how he would take down three shooters, in whichever formation they approached.

It was still light. The sun was close to setting, and through gaps in the leaves, he could see the sky had turned orange.

He tried to look at the ridge, but there was too much foliage in his way. All he could see was a narrow section of the flats. Grass swaying lightly in the thin breeze. The chirp of birds.

He let his chi roam and summoned that grey fog. The one that enveloped him and turned him into a killing machine.

After precisely eight minutes, a shadow crossed the small area of the flats that he could see.

No human sounds. No other blocking of light.

He turned his attention to the ground beneath him, about

twenty square feet of which he could see. The tree trunk that he had climbed. Chest-high growth on all sides.

The narrow opening through which Sara and he had run.

They'll have to come through that. Any other way and their clothing will snag.

Zeb waited. It was the most natural state for him to be in.

There had been a time when he had waited thirty hours in the desert to take a kill shot.

The first sound reached him.

A step. It sounded unnaturally loud since he was so focused on that small universe of space and motion.

First came an AK's barrel. Pointing straight ahead. Below him. Then a head of thick hair appeared. Black or brown, he couldn't be sure. Tanned neck.

A second man appeared below him. Similar appearance, wearing a leather jacket.

Both men stood motionless for long moments. Assessing. Listening.

All they could hear was the forest.

A bead of sweat rolled down Zeb's nose and splashed on the branch he was perched on.

He thought it sounded like a waterfall, but knew that was his imagination.

One man nodded slightly, and they went out of sight to his right.

He didn't move.

Ten minutes later, the third man appeared. He seemed shorter, though it was hard to say from Zeb's position.

Zeb sighed in relief.

Only three men. If there had been more, the third man wouldn't be alone.

Because no shooter went alone in hostile territory. Unless he had no choice.

The third gunman was as careful as the first two.

He, too, stopped below Zeb to survey his surroundings.

He was the cover for the advance men. It was his job to take care of their six.

However, there was no one to look out for him.

Zeb jumped.

Chapter 44

He had been meaning to land squarely on the shooter's shoulders, a leg to each side of his head.

But the gunman seemed to feel the rush of motion. He turned at the last moment, so that Zeb's left thigh slammed into his hard shoulder, and his right knee smashed into the shooter's head.

Zeb grunted. He couldn't help it.

The shooter began collapsing from the sudden weight, a startled shout escaping from his throat.

It was too late for evasive action.

He was falling.

Zeb's knife was plunging into his chest.

Repeatedly.

Zeb rolled away from the bloodied shooter on the ground, his left hand flicking back to draw his Glock.

Just as the advance team crashed through the bushes.

Two pairs of startled eyes took in everything.

'*Enrico!*' One man yelled.

They sprang apart, their AKs coming up.

Their shouts were drowned out by the roll of thunder from

Zeb's Glock, which knocked back the killer to his left.

The hunting knife flew from his right hand and thudded into the right shooter's chest.

Not a clean throw.

The Glock blurred as it flew from his left to his right palm.

It cracked twice, and the second shooter went down.

Zeb rolled swiftly to the far edge of the clearing.

Checked the approach.

Clear.

The ridge, too.

He listened.

No sounds of approaching men.

He took in the three dead men.

Enrico, one of them had shouted.

They didn't look like any of Namir's men that he had seen.

Tavez's shooters, then. That means the cartel king and the terrorist have joined hands.

Tavez probably knows the forest.

There will be more men after us.

He didn't spend any time thinking about this development. It was what it was.

'Tulip!' he yelled, as he dragged the bodies and hid them under bushes. He removed spare mags, another hunting knife, and their wallets.

He found no cellphones.

He covered the bodies carefully. Sara Ashland had seen enough death in her life.

No need for her to see more dead shooters.

'Tulip!' he shouted again.

'I am here.' She came from behind him, her teeth biting her lip when she saw the state of his leg.

But she said nothing.

She helped him gather the AKs and then stopped when he exclaimed: 'That isn't an AK 47. Things happened so fast, I didn't pay attention. It's an M24 SWS, Sniper Weapon System.'

He tested the rifle's heft, fingered its stock and peered through its scope.

'Good condition, too.'

'One of the men was a sniper?' She slung the other AK 47 around her shoulder and shrugged when he stared at her. 'What? You said we can't have too many weapons.'

She bent and pocketed the spare magazines on the ground.

Her steely façade disappeared when they heard shouts from the ridge.

She came closer to him instinctively.

'Are those…?'

He crept forward and hid behind one of the bushes, the girl behind him.

He raised the M24 to his eye and took in view of the slope.

'Yeah. Three of them.'

'I didn't know Namir had a sniper.'

'He didn't. Tavez has joined him.'

He felt her shiver as he lay down and brought the rifle to his shoulder.

It felt comfortable, the stock warm against his cheek, as if he had used the weapon for a long time.

'What are you doing?'

'Discouraging them.'

Chapter 45

Zeb's first shot sent one of the terrorists tumbling down the slope. He lay still when he reached the bottom.

The second shot spun another man around, but he managed to scramble across the ridge to safety.

'I thought you would be a great shot,' the girl said. 'You seem to be good at everything else.'

The third terrorist wasn't hanging around. He had dived behind the slope when the first man went down.

'It's my leg, ma'am. If I was uninjured …'

She snorted, 'And what's with the ma'am? Sara. That's my name.'

'It's the way I am, ma'am.'

He heard her sigh, but she didn't respond.

They lay still for several moments, watching, but no heads appeared over the slope.

'Let's go.'

He examined her as she gave him a hand and helped him up.

There was dirt on her clothes. The rubber tube was sticking out of a pocket. The knife was jammed in her belt.

Her face was wan, her eyes tired, and her lips had developed an unconscious tremble.

'What about them?' She pointed to the ridge.

'They now know we have the sniper rifle. That will make them think.'

'What will they do?'

'They will circle around,' he said, pointing to the ridge line. 'Will try to surround us. Try to stop us before we get to the Middle Fork Salmon River.'

'Why? They can stop us after we cross, can't they?'

'Yeah. But with that M24, it would be easier for us to pick them off as they crossed. If we hung around.'

She turned without a word and started running. In the direction of the river.

They didn't slacken their pace, even though his leg felt like his thigh bones were grinding together.

At eight pm, he called a halt.

'We can't run blindly in the dark,' he told her.

She leaned against a tree and slid down it as if she were boneless, huffing loudly.

He made a small fire from sticks, using Koeman's matchsticks.

He broke open cans from his pack and sharpened a twig for her to use as a fork.

'Why did you make the fire if you aren't going to heat anything?'

'A fire makes us feel better, ma'am. Always has. From the times we lived in caves.'

'Can't they see it?'

'No, ma'am,' he said, chewing some beef jerky slowly. 'That's why I picked this spot. Trees around us. Fire less than a foot high. Branches to break the smoke streams.'

'They can smell the fire.'

'If they are close, yeah.' He emptied his can and thought of warning her about what he would do next.

Light danced on her face and turned it soft. As if she was smiling.

She has seen worse.

He got to his feet and stripped off his combat trousers.

He unsheathed his knife and heated it in the flame.

He poured water into her empty can and placed it over the fire.

'Yes, ma'am. I've got to do it.' He read the question in her eyes.

And dug the hot blade into his thigh.

Chapter 46

Zeb bit down hard on the collar of his jacket, but despite that, a deep groan escaped him.

He shook his head to dislodge the sweat from his eyes and opened the wound in his thigh.

'Please look away, ma'am,' he gasped.

She came closer instead and put a hand on his shoulder.

His wound was dark in the light, blood pouring down his thigh, falling to the ground.

He bit his tongue when the knife reached the bullet, molten lava flowing through him.

More probing and digging until he finally got the knife tip underneath it.

The misshapen round finally fell into the empty can with a *clink*. He lay back, panting for a moment, and then heaved himself upright.

He washed his wound with water, cut more strips from his T-shirt and bound the thigh tight.

There was no way to stop the bleeding completely. The wound wasn't like the furrow on his shoulder.

His thigh would keep leaking blood till he could get to a

medic.'

He washed his hands, wiped his face, and drank greedily from the canteen.

The crackle of flames was the only sound in the forest until Sara Ashland reached for the can and shook it.

The bullet rolled from side to side until she stilled the container.

'Will you die?'

Her eyes looked haunted, shining with unshed tears.

He held back from answering, fingering the crude bandage around his thigh, already damp from seeping blood.

He tore another strip and tightened it around his leg.

He could hear himself breathing. Loud and harsh.

He would die. He was sure of that. All Namir and Tavez had to do was attack them in full strength.

They would kick his body and dance on it.

He stood and tested his leg. It would hold. It would carry him for as long as there was breath in him.

He brushed grains of soil from his fingers. Felt a cool wind drift and dry the sweat on his face.

Earth. Wind. Fire. Water.

Many cultures believe all creation came from those elements. On dying, the human body dissolves into them.

He crouched in front of her, ignoring the stab of pain that shot through him.

He made a vow to himself. He wouldn't die just yet.

'You will live. You will be safe with your granddad. I promise.'

She didn't say anything. She sat silently, looking at him. As if feeling his words, weighing them, letting them settle inside her.

At last she nodded. Her palm reached out and gripped his forearm once. Tightly.

'I feel safe with you.'

He kept watch as she slept and the wilderness slumbered, too.

Her soft breathing reached him.

Her face relaxed and became that of the teenager.

I feel safe with you.

He rose, blood pulsing inside him, taking oxygen from alveoli, feeding it to the darkness inside him, bringing it to life.

He looked deep into the distance, in the direction of their pursuers, and as a wolf howled somewhere, in that split second, with the moon casting its dim glow, Zeb Carter knew what he had to do.

He became the most dangerous predator to prowl the wilderness.

Chapter 47

He woke her at three am on Thursday.

The fire had died out and darkness had enveloped their camp.

She stretched and yawned and stiffened when reality and her surroundings hit her.

'Are they here?' she asked nervously.

'No. But I would like to get to the river by dawn.'

She got up swiftly without complaint. Shook the dirt off her clothes.

Shouldered her AK 47 and helped him fasten the HKs and the M24 around his back.

'Can you see? To make our way?'

'There's enough light,' he said, pointing to the top. 'Your eyes will get used to it.'

She swirled water in her mouth, swallowed it, and started walking in the direction he indicated.

'Ma'am.'

'Yeah?'

'I am not with the FBI.'

She stopped and turned sideways at him.

'I am a Special Forces operative. With a secretive unit.'

'Like one of those Delta guys?'

'Something like that. But I am not in the Army.'

Her brow wrinkled. 'Why are you telling me this? Now?'

'I have worked with the toughest men and women. We go through brutal training.'

'So?'

'None of them would have borne themselves like you have.'

'My world has ended. I am hanging by a thread,' she said and began to walk faster.

'Yes, ma'am. But those operators. They would have gone to pieces—'

'I am close to it.'

'You haven't complained. You haven't given up. You haven't argued.

'You need to know—' He was suddenly lost for words. 'It's my honor to help you. To take you back safe.' He clamped his jaws shut before he embarrassed himself further.

'Zeb?' she seemed to sniffle.

'Yes, ma'am?'

'I don't care who you are. FBI. Special Forces. Those names don't mean anything to me.'

'Yes, ma'am.'

'I am glad you are on my side.'

'Yes, ma'am.'

'Has anyone told you, you talk too much?'

'No, ma'am.'

'Well, why don't you shut up and run faster?'

'Yes, ma'am.'

They picked up speed and reached the river at six am.

It was a section where the Middle Fork Salmon River

narrowed and was thirty feet wide.

'You can swim, ma'am? I never asked you that.'

'Like a fish. Why are we hiding?'

They were still amongst the trees, which gave way abruptly to a steep descent, at the bottom of which was the river.

The slope on their side was rocky, and on the other full of gravel and small boulders.

River's calmer here. No strong currents.

Just beyond their vision, to their right, were whitewater rapids.

There would be no rafts or canoeists that early in the morning.

Which is why I wanted to arrive early. If Namir or Tavez are here, it would have put them at risk.

He looked at the slope with narrowed eyes.

Ten minutes to get to the river.

Twenty minutes to cross it.

Another ten minutes to climb the bank and get into cover.

In all, forty minutes in the open.

No signs of pursuit.

His radar didn't ping.

'Let's go.'

She took off at a run.

'Slow down,' he urged her, when she slipped on a rock.

Can't risk broken limbs.

She heeded, and climbed down carefully.

He waited till she was at the bottom, and then started.

Gritted his teeth as his injured thigh protested.

He carefully picked the rocks where he would place his feet, and was so intent on his descent that he didn't hear the approach.

It was her scream that warned him.
He whirled around.
And went down as a body slammed into him.
The hostile's hand rose.
A knife plunged toward him.

Chapter 48

'He killed Enrico,' the gunman snarled as he paced the Mexican cartel's camp.

Six of the gang were sprawled on the ground, while three others served sentry duty.

Joachim Tavez whittled on a stick with a sharp blade, half-listening to the enraged Julio.

Julio had a right to be furious. Enrico was his younger brother.

The two had been with Tavez ever since the cartel was formed.

Now, Enrico was dead and the older sibling wanted revenge.

Revenge for a gang member's killing didn't figure high on Tavez's list of priorities. What mattered was that no affront went unpunished.

The stranger had killed Hector, Enrico, and Gomes.

Gomes. That made the cartel boss burn. That man had been the best shooter in Mexico. Rival cartels had attempted to hire him. When that failed, they had tried to kill him.

Gomes had shot up their killers and, after that, there had

been no more trouble.

Not only were three of his men dead, there was the fact that the stranger and the girl knew of the farm.

Both had to die.

But Tavez couldn't help marveling how the stranger had taken out his men. Even a wounded leg hadn't stopped him.

'Are we going to do something?' Julio challenged.

Tavez looked up and subdued his man with a cold stare.

'We are.' A shooter brought him coffee in a plastic cup and waited for him to finish it.

The drug lord tossed it back to him carelessly and focused on Julio.

'We are doing what we agreed.'

His glare reduced the dissenter to sullen silence.

Leopard. That was the name the bearded stranger gave.

Tavez knew that wasn't his real name. He also knew the man and his shooters were from the Middle East. That was obvious from their accents.

Only one kind of person came from the Middle East loaded with weapons and hunting people: a terrorist.

Tavez didn't care. Leopard and his paths had converged, and for the moment, they had common goals.

Leopard had lost one of his own shooters on the slope. The American had successfully taken an incredible shot from nearly a thousand yards away.

Tavez and Leopard had held back for several hours after the killing on the slope. No one had much appetite to go up against this stranger, with his deadly prowess.

So when night fell, Leopard had proposed a new plan: He and his nine men would take a separate route.

They would go to Erilyn, or close to it.

RUN!

Cut the stranger and the girl from the front.
Tavez would come from the rear.
And the two runners would be trapped.

Chapter 49

The cartel killers had taken up the hunt in the night, cautiously, for the stranger had proven to be a deadly fighter.

Tavez knew the man and the girl were heading to the river. He knew the rough direction they were heading.

He also knew the man couldn't run at full speed. Gomes had put a bullet in his left leg.

How far can they go in the dark?

Hence, he had called a halt after an hour.

And that's when Enrico's brother had started ranting.

Julio rose when snores filled the forest. Tavez was slumped against a tree. The other shooters were scattered on the ground. All asleep.

He knew where the guards were.

Tavez had confiscated his guns, suspecting he might break from the group, go seeking vengeance on his own.

He was right, Julio thought bitterly.

But I need to avenge Enrico. And Joachim doesn't seem bothered. Otherwise he wouldn't sleep.

Julio did have a knife. He thought of stealing a gun from

one of the sleeping men. Or knocking one of the sentries out cold and taking his weapon.

But the risk was too great.

He ghosted out of the camp and picked up his pace when he thought he was out of earshot.

He ran when he could and slowed to a trot when the terrain and the darkness made it difficult to go faster.

He stopped occasionally to listen, but heard nothing.

When the forest thickened, he drew out his knife and imagined sinking it into the stranger.

Maybe he would have his way with the girl.

He was no longer beholden to Joachim. Not now.

He was on his own.

He knew Tavez would kill him, slowly, if he returned to the cartel.

That didn't scare him, either.

Revenge alone fueled him and drew him onwards in the night.

He stopped just twice. Once to drink water from a rainwater pool. And then to lean against a tree and sleep for fifteen minutes. While standing up.

Because if he sat down, he would sleep too long. And the stranger would get away.

He checked his direction several times.

West.

In the direction of the river.

Tavez had briefed them on where its waters were the calmest in that area.

The stranger would head there.

He had no choice.

And so would Julio. Because where the two escapees

went, Julio would go.

He came upon them in the most unexpected way.

He was running almost blindly, exhaustion gripping him.

The new day had dawned, and a dim light was filling the forest.

Not much, but there was more visibility.

He nearly lost his balance when the trees gave way abruptly to a steep downward slope filled with rocks.

He recovered from his near fall.

And heard voices.

He blinked stupidly, his brain not yet processing what his eyes saw.

There was the river. Smooth and serene.

And there was the girl, right at the river's bank, the stranger behind her, still descending.

Julio was flooded with rage.

As if by magic, his knife appeared in his hand.

He slithered and stumbled his way down, dislodging several rocks.

The girl heard him. Screamed in warning when she saw him.

Too late.

Julio was already flying, landing on Zeb, bringing him down.

His knife stabbing downwards.

Chapter 50

Zeb couldn't react in time.

He was half-turned when Julio's body slammed into him.

He fell on his right shoulder. Rolled so that he lay on his back.

Instinctively brought his right hand up to block the knife.

Gritted his teeth, pouring all his strength into warding off its killing strike.

Sweat fell on him, dripping from the attacker's face.

The man was screaming, yelling.

Zeb heard something about killing Enrico.

Mexican. Tavez's man.

Something struck him on the left shoulder. Right on the wound.

He groaned but didn't yield, his wrist firmly blocking the assailant's knife hand.

Rocks pricked his back. The three rifles strapped to him dug into his flesh.

His injured leg burned like it had been dipped in hot oil.

Still, he didn't yield.

If I die, she dies.

I made her a promise.

Something moved at the edge of his vision.

The girl.

Approaching them.

Swinging her AK.

'Stay out,' he grunted.

She held back.

The attacker eased off a fraction to look up, presenting an opening for Zeb.

He lunged and bit the man's ear.

The Mexican howled and struggled to get free.

Zeb didn't let up.

He kept yanking with his teeth and simultaneously smashing Julio's knife hand on the rocks.

The weapon fell away.

The attacker didn't give up or try to get away.

He punched Zeb hard on the chest. Hauled back to aim a blow at his face.

Zeb was in the zone.

His vision was sharp. His senses were acute.

He was pinned down still. The threat level was still high.

But the savage fighter in him had surfaced.

With his forearm, he deflected the incoming blow.

Jabbed at the enemy's eyes.

Drew an agonized bellow from him.

Punched the throat.

The scream choked away.

With a massive heave, Zeb threw the man away.

Followed through with a roundhouse punch.

Smashed an elbow into the attacker's ribs and heard a sharp crack above the ensuing shriek.

Julio kicked out.

Thrashed out wildly.

Zeb evaded the blows easily.

Pinned him down by leaning on his waist.

A slap rocked the assailant's face to the left.

Another sent it rolling to the right.

Zeb knew a slap was one of the most potent strikes in a fighter's arsenal. Landed correctly, with power, it could wreak tremendous damage.

It was also an insolent blow. It signified contempt.

Domination over an attacker.

That was the effect Zeb was going for.

'Who are you?' he grunted in Spanish.

The hitter's eyes flickered. Surprise, mixed with anger and fear.

'You killed Enrico,' he growled, and tried to go on the offense.

Another slap shook several of his teeth loose and split his lips.

'Ma'am,' Zeb called out, 'start swimming!'

'But—'

'Ma'am, *start swimming.*'

Zeb risked a quick glance when he heard splashing.

Sara Ashland was in the water, moving with powerful strokes.

He pressed a thumb on the attacker's neck, at a pressure point that made the gunman's body shudder.

'It's question time.'

Chapter 51

Zeb didn't kill Julio.

Instead, he dislocated both his shoulders and tied his ankles together with his shoelaces.

One last time, before plunging into the water, he looked up the bank.

Julio said Tavez and his men are a few hours away. They were sleeping when he left.

The cold water braced him, revived him. Made him temporarily forget the throbbing in his body.

His swim was a slow crawl, his eyes on the girl as she clambered onto the bank opposite and waited for him.

He raised an arm and pointed at the trees.

A burst of warmth flooded him when she hustled towards their protection.

She would fit in well with the twins. Beth, Meghan—she's just like them.

Not letting grief weigh her down.

A darker thought entered his mind.

We have been moving almost nonstop since she escaped from Namir. She's had no time to process her father's death.

He turned on his back to look back. No hostile presence.

He slowed down even further as he approached the bank.

The bottom of the river was uneven.

He had to place his feet carefully.

Can't afford a sprain. Not on top of a bad thigh.

He shook himself like a dog when he was out of the water.

Checked the two HKs and the M24.

They were badly scratched, but not bent.

His Glocks were wet; however, they would work.

His knives were tight around his right leg.

All weapons intact.

He climbed the bank and, when he was under the shade of trees, she came from behind a ponderosa.

'Took you long enough,' she quipped, her eyes not reflecting her light tone.

She looked him up and down, her eyes lingering on the dark bandage on his leg.

'I was fighting, ma'am. In case you didn't notice.'

'I thought you Special Ops folks could deal with such men with one hand.'

'I have just one hand and one leg, ma'am.'

'What did he say?'

'I am waiting.' Impatient. A hand on her hip, when he didn't reply immediately.

'Tavez has joined forces with Namir.'

Chapter 52

He turned his back around when she removed the AK and unzipped her hoodie.

He heard her strip and wring water out of her clothes.

'That's not good.'

He looked over his shoulder, then turned when she had shrugged back into her hoodie.

'No, ma'am.'

Enrico said Namir introduced himself as Leopard. That's proof, if I needed it. That's the escaped war criminal, hunting us.

'We should get out of here,' she snapped impatiently when he made no move.

'I am tired of running.'

A vein throbbed on her neck.

A splash from the river.

Fish. Arcing in the air and falling gracefully.

'You're suggesting we fight both gangs?' she asked, incredulous.

'Namir—he and his men aren't behind us.'

'They've given up?'

'No. They are heading to Erilyn. To attack us from that direction.'

She chewed her lips as he tore yet another strip off his T-shirt and used it to clean his weapons.

When he held a hand out, she gave him the AK and watched as he expertly dismantled it, wiped each part, and put it back together.

'You can do that in the dark?' she asked absentmindedly.

'Yes, ma'am.'

And blindfolded.

'How many men does Tavez have?'

'He had eleven. Now, seven.'

'And Namir?'

'Ten. That was one of his men that I shot.'

'They won't give up?' A forlorn hope in her voice.

'No, ma'am.'

'You have a plan?'

'Sort of.'

His plan consisted of waiting.

He figured the cartel would take the same route as Julio had.

This was one of the calmer spots in the river.

If I were Tavez, I would come here.

He found a good shooting site: a natural depression in the ground, bushes to cover him, and boulders that he rolled over it, to shield him.

He was above, the river below.

Firing angle was from high to low.

Very little wind.

Great visibility.

Good shooting conditions.

He chewed on a piece of beef jerky as he settled down to wait, Sara Ashland next to him, taking on the role of spotter.

He had asked her to go farther back. Make herself comfortable. Catch some sleep.

Her lip had curled stubbornly in the manner he had come to recognize.

Never go against an obstinate teenager.

The sun climbed into the sky and beat down on them as the minutes became hours.

He heard her breathing slow and turn into the rhythm of sleep, but didn't stop his vigil.

It was late afternoon when she stirred, brushed hair from her eyes and stifled a yawn.

She watched, mouth agape, as he stood up and slung the M24 behind him.

'What? Aren't you going to shoot them as they come?'

'They aren't coming.'

Chapter 53

'How do you know that?' Sara Ashland hurried to catch up with Zeb as he strode into the forest.

He took his time replying.

He was thinking of the area's map. The river curled around an outcropping and disappeared from view. Whitewater, out of their sight.

'They would have come by now. Tavez won't risk a crossing in the night. They have found some other place to cross.'

'So, both teams are ahead of us?' she asked fearfully.

'Not necessarily. They have the same problem that we have. They don't know where we are. Just as we don't know where they are.'

'So, we are going to Erilyn?'

He stopped and adjusted an HK, wiping sweat from his face.

'Not yet. We need to reduce their numbers.'

'But you don't know where they are!'

'We make them come to us.'

She screamed and dropped to the ground when his Glock leaped to his palm and he fired.

'What?' she rose shakily and looked at what he had shot.

'Food, ma'am. We'll run out of supplies soon.'

He went to the rabbit, shielding it from her with his body, and started stripping it with his knife.

Zeb took no pleasure in hunting. He usually fished for food when he was in the wilderness. However, needs had to be met.

He washed the flesh, cut it into smaller portions, and packed it in their bag.

He squinted at the sky; a few more hours to dark.

Sara Ashland fell in beside him as they resumed their fast hike.

'That shot. You didn't clean up behind us. I've noticed you always do. You're leaving a trail for them.'

'Yes, ma'am. Now to find the right place to wait.'

They found it ninety minutes later.

The forest thinned out, became a flat plain, and then turned rocky, dotted with knee-high grass and waist-high bushes.

'Here?' she asked, looking left, right, and then to the skies. 'This is right in the open. They can pick us off from a distance.'

'So can we. But this is just the bait.' He pointed.

A couple of miles in the distance, the hard ground gave way to what looked like a hole between two hills. A narrow ravine with steep, rocky sides, sparsely vegetated, with large boulders alarmingly perched above on the cliffs.

'That will be the trap.'

They jogged lightly, Zeb wincing. The girl didn't comment when she caught his expression.

They slowed them as they approached the passage between the hills, which was far narrower than it had seemed: twelve feet wide at the bottom, a dry stream bed, with craggy hills on each side rising to about two hundred feet.

The valley petered out after just half a mile, and then the forest resumed.

'Here?'

'Yes, ma'am. This will be our kill zone.'

Chapter 54

Zeb and Sara Ashland went back to the flat area and lit a fire. Not big, but large enough to be visible from the forest.

He undressed his wound and dropped some of the bloodied strips to the ground.

Made new bandages from the girl's T-shirt and bound his thigh again.

'That's for them to find?'

'Yeah. Only one of them.'

They headed back to the valley and, behind a rock near its entrance, he smudged the ground with his feet.

He placed sticks close together, the makings for a fire, and dropped the other dressing.

'They will suspect it's a trap.'

'Yes, ma'am. However, they will still come. Tavez wants us badly enough that he will risk it.'

There were loose boulders on the canyon floor, which had rolled down from the hills in the distant past.

He tested a few of them.

Some of them moved.

He heaved at one and, when the girl joined in, succeeded

in rolling it right into the center of the valley.

They shifted more rocks, placing them strategically throughout the passage.

'That,' he said, brushing his hands against his trousers, 'will slow them down. It will split them up. The strength in numbers that they have ... they will lose that.'

'Where will we be? This will become too small for all of us.'

'Up there,' he pointed to the cliff face on their left.

It was almost barren. No vegetation. Clumps of stone and rubble. A few rocks that looked like they could tip over anytime. The few trees on the cliff were widely spaced out.

'There's nothing there to shelter us,' she protested. 'That side, on the right, has more cover.'

The other slope did offer more protection. It was uneven. Hollows and bushes. Several firs. There was one particular spot that Zeb liked—a large slab of stone, underneath which was a hole through which they could see the sky.

'Tavez will expect us to be there,' he countered. 'There won't be an element of surprise.'

They climbed the barren slope and made a cold camp behind the largest stone.

In a small, natural depression.

Behind them, the hill rose, pointing defiantly at the sky.

The hollow shields us from the top. It reduces our view, too, but that's a chance I'll take.

The downstream shooting angle was good. Visibility was still good.

He broke open a can of food and handed it to her.

They ate quickly, using the knives to spear the dried meat slices. He buried the can and waited.

RUN!

M24 to his shoulder. One HK and both Glocks beside him. Ready to take on the Mexican cartel. Reduce the odds. Joachim Tavez surprised him.

Chapter 55

Zeb knew his plan had failed when he heard the sound.

It was eight pm. A dark sky. A few stars and a distant moon.

The slopes were full of shadows, as was the ravine. No movement down below.

However, his ears had pricked and he had gone to full alert.

It was a slither he had heard, the sound of clothing scraping against rock.

From behind them.

He strained his ears, opening his eyes as wide as possible to take in light.

Nope. Nothing below.

There! The sound came again.

From above them on the hillside.

Sara Ashland was sleeping beside him. He didn't wake her.

He moved slowly. Face turning. Left elbow coming up to cover its paleness.

Waited for his eyes to adjust.

Saw nothing but the rim of their depression. A few trees beyond it. A large rock.

Then the sound again.
Closer, this time.
Probably twenty feet away.
Now, a clatter of stones.
A sudden absence of noise.
Zeb couldn't help grinning.
Someone had been careless. And had now frozen.
Long moments passed.
A scrape.
Something broke the skyline.
A head.
To his right.
A body appeared.
Something gleaming in the light.
A rifle pointed forward.
The shooter inched forward, his eyes straight ahead, peering at the valley below.
Another head to Zeb's left.
At the edge of his vision.
The second hitter, too, was intent on the ravine.
Why didn't they spot our hollow?
He rifled through his memory, remembering the topography.
Maybe from the top it appears to be even ground.
The two men passed him.
He waited for interminable minutes.
No further movement from the top.
These two are scouts? An advance team to check the valley?
They now appeared below him.
Still moving slowly.

Crouching slightly. Placing their feet with care.
Another thought intruded.
They could be hikers.
He snapped a glance behind him.
No more hitters.
He considered his options.
The girl was safest where she was.
There were two rocks, far to his right. They would offer cover if needed.
He grabbed a handful of loose soil and tossed it to his right, into the valley.
The two shooters reacted instantly.
They dropped and shot in the direction of the sound.
Not hikers.
The girl awoke.
He cupped a palm over her mouth.
She nodded.
Stay here.
She bobbed her head again.
He brought the M24 to his shoulder.
Sighted.
Pulled the trigger smoothly till it broke.
Inched the barrel. Took a shot at the second man.
Rose to a crouch. Ran to the distant rock he had seen to his right.
Saw the fallen shooters move.
So, mine weren't kill shots.
Threw himself to the ground, the rifle coming up automatically.
Triggered rapidly.
Two shots into the left body mass, two more into the right.

Heard their agonized screams.
Saw them thrashing.
He didn't move.
No other fighters appeared on the skyline.
He waited, then made an instinctive decision.
He descended to the valley.

Chapter 56

Zeb raced down, swerving randomly to throw off any shooters.
No rounds came his way.
He was nearing the shooter on the right when … *they aren't down!*
Both fallen men moved suddenly, rolling onto their backs.
Zeb couldn't stop his forward motion.
Ten feet separated him from the closest killer.
Fifteen from the second.
Time slowed.
He heard one of them grunt as he brought his rifle up.
The other, the more distant one, was quicker.
He triggered.
A round flew into the sky harmlessly.
Zeb flung himself to his left.
His Glock came up.
A snapped shot before he landed.
The nearest hitter jerked.
Zeb fell on his left shoulder.
The Glock didn't waver.
It was the middle of a geometric line starting from Zeb's

eyes and ending at the second killer's body mass.

Trigger pull.

Turn.

Another shot at the first.

Rounds whistling around him. One grazing his cheek.

He fired twice more.

Someone groaned.

No return fire.

A body twitched.

Zeb twisted to his right.

Got to his feet.

Zigged to the left.

Took two steps forward.

Zagged.

Shooter close to him twitched. His hand tried to lift his rifle.

Zeb shot him.

Went to the second man, who was on his back.

His eyes blinking slowly.

His chest a mass of wetness.

Zeb kicked away his weapon.

Kneeled next to him.

Put his Glock to his temple.

'Where are the others?'

Movement behind him.

Zeb sprang away, turning in mid-flight, gun coming up.

It was Sara Ashland.

'Ma'am, that's a good way to get killed,' he gasped, sliding on gravel.

'Did he say anything?'

'It's best you move away.'

Zeb didn't want her to see the man die, but the girl didn't budge.

She sat next to him.

'Where is Tavez?'

'Go away,' his voice flat, hard.

'I have seen dead men. Dying people.'

'Go.'

She rose in a huff and walked away. Her rigid back showing her displeasure.

'Is Tavez coming?' he asked in Spanish.

'No …' the hitter sighed, blinking slowly. 'Other side.'

'Other side of the hill? Which hill?'

The cartel man nodded jerkily and moaned when Zeb pointed to the slope they had come down.

'Tavez went ahead.'

Another nod.

It struck Zeb.

'If you returned alive, we would be dead. If not, Tavez would be waiting?'

'Yessss.'

Chapter 57

Zeb sat with the shooter till he stopped breathing. Even one who had tried to kill him didn't need to die alone.

'Are more coming?' Sara Ashland asked him sharply.

'No. They went ahead. They'll be waiting once we get out of the valley.'

'We've got to go.' She plucked his sleeve urgently. 'Find a different route.'

'No.'

'No?' Her voice rose.

'That's what he'll be expecting. For all we know, he has divided his men. Some on that hill, others with him. They can trap us.'

'We do nothing?'

'We wait right here.' He started climbing, back to the hollow they had occupied.

'He'll come in the night,' she hissed in anger.

'No, ma'am. Tavez is down to six men. He knows his killers failed. He will not risk another attempt. Not in the valley. And not in the dark.'

'What do we do now?'

'I don't know about you, ma'am. But I intend to sleep.'

His eyes flew open at five am on Friday. Blue skies high above.

Clouds going about their way, lazily.

An orange glow to the east.

They had survived another night.

He didn't move, thinking about their enemies.

Joachim Tavez with four men.

Ten terrorists, somewhere far ahead.

Why did Namir go to Erilyn? Or in that direction?

He knows we are heading that way, he answered himself.

Yeah, but the closer he gets to town, the higher the risk for him.

He pondered it for several moments and then gave up, with an impatient shake of his head.

Who knew how terrorists thought?

There's something else. Something I am not getting.

He stretched and rose.

Dragged the bodies away and hid them as best he could, under a bush.

Washed his face and lit a small fire.

He boiled water and was brewing coffee when she woke up.

'Dad?' she called and sat up and yawned.

Her eyes fell on him.

Her face fell as reality hit.

He thrust a cup at her.

'We move at six.'

He led them down the valley, aware that she was searching for the dead men.

'Thank you,' she said softly when they were at the bottom.

'For not letting me see,' she made a face as if he should know why, when he quirked an eyebrow.

'We're going up there?' She kept pace when he started climbing the other slope.

He nodded his head.

'Just as easy to die on another hill.'

Teenager-with-attitude was back.

Chapter 58

They didn't die on the incline. They didn't even meet any gunmen.

Just means Tavez is further ahead. Waiting for us.

As they neared the top, he dropped to the ground and started crawling.

Because there was nothing to protect them on the summit, just a rounding of the ground, and then the descent began.

He scoped the downhill slope.

More trees this side, for which he was thankful.

But they thinned when they reached the flats.

'We'll walk in the trees. The thickest part, over there,' he pointed. 'Follow the line around the side of the hill. Sprint when we reach that grassy land at the front. Until we get into the forest.'

She wet her lips and followed his arm.

'We're in the right direction? To Erilyn?'

'Yes, ma'am. Though we have lost time.'

She started rising.

He grabbed her leg.

'Crawl, ma'am. We are on the downhill. We'll be exposed against the skyline.'

Going down was hard.

They slipped on loose gravel, their weapons making the descent hard.

She didn't whine.

Not even when she banged her head against a rock after losing grip.

He caught hold of her, steadied her, and they resumed.

We would have been sitting ducks if Tavez had showed up.

He got up cautiously, using tree trunks to shield him.

Listened to the forest for any movement.

Something rattled in the bushes.

His Glock came out in a flash.

A rattlesnake slithered out, its forked tongue darting.

They stood motionless while it wriggled away behind them and melted into the undergrowth.

'I had never seen a snake before coming to America.' Sara unscrewed a water canteen and drank. 'I couldn't stop screaming when I saw my first one. Near our home. Dad took me camping whenever he could. I got used to wildlife. Now …'

She jammed the container on her hip and marched ahead.

He didn't know what to say. He had never been a conversationalist.

I was once. When I had a wife. A child.

'Slow, ma'am. The hills might have eyes,' he cautioned her.

She tossed her head, but reduced her pace.

He directed her a few times, because the slope wasn't a straight line down.

It undulated. There were hollows and small rises.

They chose a depression and cut a trail through its thickest growth.

Not stopping, not flagging, because he wanted to cover as many miles as possible that day, get as close to the town as they could.

She'll be safe tomorrow. When we reach Erilyn.

Maybe he, too, was exhausted. Or was careless.

Because he didn't hear anything to warn him.

He didn't register a footfall or any movement around them before he felt the round whiz past his forehead.

It thudded into a tree trunk—bark flying and smacking into his face.

Instinct and training took over.

He was moving even before he knew what was happening.

His left hand slammed into her back.

Sent her sprawling ahead.

While he leaped behind.

Both of them falling.

Just as more rounds struck.

Throwing up soil and stones.

Where he had been just a moment ago.

Chapter 59

Zeb looked behind him.

No shooter in sight. Not yet.

He looked below, his vision restricted by the hollow.

The downhill slope extended for another hundred yards below them.

He couldn't hear any footsteps in that direction.

The rifle opened up again and raked the top of their hollow.

He saw Sara cover, trying to make herself smaller.

She was just five feet away.

Looking back at him, scared.

Move forward, he mouthed. *Get away from me.*

She inched ahead.

He wriggled back.

And stopped when a round pierced through the soil and nearly creased his shoulder.

No cover behind me.

The hollow ends.

The depression was small.

Maybe a foot and a half deep.

Just enough to protect their bodies.

The shooter had all the advantages.

He could keep on firing until the soil broke.

He could then pick them off.

Zeb lunged up when the rifle stopped to snatch a look.

Ducked back.

Trees. No hitter in the open.

However, behind one fir a barrel had been sticking out.

About ten feet away.

Close. Very close. Couldn't see another shooter.

Only one rifle firing at us.

He shifted slightly to ease the hard press of the rifles on his back.

Got an idea.

Holstered the Glock that had leaped into his hand when he was diving.

Reached behind carefully.

Shrank when a round sang into the air, over his body.

Dug himself deeper into the ground and reached back again.

Grabbed one HK and twisted it up and around till he could hold it.

'Gringo.'

He froze.

'I know you are there.' The voice sounded cheerful. English with a Mexican accent.

'We found Julio. He was alive. Joachim killed him. He has no use for an injured man.'

He spat and let loose another volley, raining mud and stones on Zeb.

'We also found Torres. And Loya. Both were my friends.'

'I have time, gringo,' he chuckled. 'Where you are hiding.

That won't hide you forever. Then I will kill you. And that girl …' He smacked his lips loudly.

'I will play with her.'

'Then I will give her to Joachim.'

Zeb saw Sara shiver and crawl forward another foot.

A thought nagged him.

This dude didn't need to announce his intention.

He could have kept firing and our cover would have collapsed.

He's sounding confident.

He's got backup?

A stick cracked.

He twisted his head.

Cold washed over him when he saw a second shooter come into view.

Below them.

Six or seven feet away.

AK casually but firmly gripped.

Heading towards Sara.

Chapter 60

The sight triggered muscles that powered Zeb to explosive action.

He dug his feet into the hard ground.

Sprang out of the cover, his core muscles, calves and thighs pistoning him out like an arrow.

Body in a straight line.

Presenting the smallest possible target to the shooter.

Flying toward the second attacker.

Zeb's HK opened up as he fired at the shooter behind the tree, pinning him down with two bursts.

The gunman opened up blindly from behind his tree.

A round burned Zeb's hip.

Another whistled past his neck.

Something tugged at his trouser leg, and his shoe felt as it if it had been kicked.

He blocked everything out, keeping only the positions of the hitters in his mind.

His rifle swiveled in his hand.

He fired it blindly over his head.

Toward the second man.

Into whom he crashed seconds later, both of them going down and into another hollow.

Out of sight of the first shooter.

He turned sideways and smashed the butt of the HK in the killer's face.

Followed up with a second blow to the throat.

A third, savage blow to the head.

The hitter groaned.

Silence fell in the forest.

The tree shooter fired savagely, blindly raking the ground with long bursts.

I hope Sara keeps her head down.

Zeb couldn't see her.

But knew where she was.

To his left. In the front.

Just after the depression they had sheltered in.

She seemed to read his mind.

Her hand rose for a second.

Her fingers waggled.

Then disappeared.

The man beneath him stirred.

Zeb slipped off him.

Jammed the barrel against his neck.

'Cesar,' the tree shooter called out.

Cesar opened his eyes.

Blinked.

Realization flooded him when Zeb jabbed him.

I got him, Zeb mouthed, and his finger tightened on the trigger.

Cesar swallowed. Sweat beaded his forehead.

'I got him,' he croaked.

'You what?'

'I got him,' he yelled, more confidently. 'In the chest. He is not moving.'

Zeb nodded approvingly.

'Are you sure?'

'Of course, I am sure, you fool.' Cesar embellished. 'The girl is hiding. A few feet away.'

'Get her then.'

'I can't. He shot me in the leg. Grab her. Then help me.'

Silence.

'All right.'

Zeb reared up just as the tree shooter stepped out.

He fired.

His rounds went wide.

He corrected just as the shooter dived to the ground, bringing his AK up.

He was too late.

Zeb's burst of fire flung his body back and took him out of the fight.

Cesar moved, slithering away.

Zeb was expecting it.

He twisted and struck like a snake, the full weight of his HK catching the hitter flush in the mouth, knocking him out.

Zeb took several moments to get his breath back.

A few seconds of action had felt like an hour.

He got to his feet and found Sara regarding him quizzically.

'Just how many lives do you have?'

Chapter 61

Zeb hauled Cesar up and, with Sara's help, bound him to a tree.

The hitter came to, slowly, groaning, his eyes flying open when he found he couldn't move.

He strained his bonds and twisted as he tried to free himself.

He started cursing when Zeb walked to him. Spat and missed.

Zeb blocked the girl's view with his body and dug a thumb into Cesar's thigh.

He stiffened, turned white, and trembled.

Sweat popped on his face. His mouth opened but no sound came.

He gasped and slumped when Zeb released him.

'Where is he?' Zeb asked him.

Cesar groaned.

Zeb raised his hand.

The shooter flinched.

'Pool,' he mumbled.

'What pool?'

'He will kill you,' the captive snarled. 'Slowly. He will share that girl with—'

He screamed when Zeb pressed the nerve again.

'I'll feed you to the vultures if you don't tell me.'

Cesar shrank when he saw the cold, implacable face in front of him. Read something swirling in the hard, brown eyes.

'There's a large pool. Almost a lake,' he said, jerking his shoulder in the direction of Erilyn. 'Joachim said he will wait there. Until noon today.'

'Describe it. Where exactly is it?'

The Mexican gave halting answers.

The cartel knew the forest well. They had to, if they were going to use it to grow their pot.

The pond was five miles away. Beyond the valley, in wilderness. In the same direction Zeb had been heading to.

'What's so special about it?'

'Trees and rocks,' the shooter said wearily. 'Well protected. No one can go to it without making a sound.'

His eyes grew mean. 'I am sure he heard the shots. He will know you are coming.'

'Why? It could be you, not us.'

Cesar shook his head knowingly. 'We were to fire in the air. Three long bursts. If we killed you.'

'Where's Namir?'

'Who?'

'That other man. Leopard. And his men.'

A calculating light entered the killer's eyes. And disappeared just as fast when Zeb unsheathed his knife.

'Gone. To Erilyn. To stop you from there.'

'He told you why he was hunting us?'

'No. He said he wanted the girl.'

That tallies with Enrico's story.

'Joachim believed him?'

'Tavez believes no one,' Cesar proudly defended his boss. 'But we, too, wanted you. You won't get away. You will die. She, too. Eventually.'

Zeb didn't reply.

He turned his back on the Mexican and picked up the fallen AKs.

He smashed them against trees. Checked that neither Cesar nor the dead shooter had any cell on them.

'What about me?' the bound man yelled when he and Sara started walking away.

'You will die,' he replied, without breaking a stride.

'Eventually.'

Chapter 62

The burn on Zeb's hip turned out to be a red, angry stripe from left to right.

It wasn't deep and, other than mild discomfort, didn't hinder his movement.

There was a hole in his right trouser leg, just beneath the calf, and one of his shoe heels was missing.

They had stripped Cesar of his shirt, paying no attention to the shooter's protests.

'We need it for bandages,' Sara told the hitter, helpfully. 'Think of it as the one good deed in your life.'

They stopped when they were beyond his hearing.

The girl wrinkled her nose at the odor coming off the garment, and tore a length of it.

She helped Zeb dress his thigh and shoulder and clean up the welt on his hip.

'He was right. Tavez will have heard the shots. What do you think he will do?' her fingers worked deftly as they tightened the bandages.

'He will be waiting. He will set a trap.'

'We can avoid that pond. The forest is big enough.'

'No,' Zeb shook his head, his face grim. 'He will just

follow us. Attack us from behind.'

'You have a plan?'

'Nope.'

They took their time.

They halted several times: food breaks, water breaks. Sleep breaks.

'He'll be under pressure,' Zeb explained when Sara looked askance at him during their second stop. 'He will be expecting us to go to the pond promptly. The more we delay, the more impatient he will get.'

'He will make mistakes.'

'Yeah.'

It was late afternoon when they smelled the stench.

'Dead water. Stagnant,' he whispered.

They couldn't see the pool yet. The forest had thickened, obscuring their view.

The ground was flat, but beyond, they could see another craggy rise.

The pond seemed to be at the base of the incline.

Waist-high bushes tugged at their clothing as they made their way carefully.

Dead leaves beneath their feet.

They started crawling.

It was slow going, since an HK was in Zeb's left hand, and his thigh was complaining.

The smell grew stronger, and when Zeb carefully parted the vegetation, they saw the pond: fifty feet across, irregular in shape.

A couple of feet of open ground surrounding it before the forest took over.

Dark, still water.

A dead bird floating on it.

Shadows speckled with sunlight.

No sign of Joachim Tavez or any of his men.

He motioned at the girl and started moving, circling the water from the left.

'Are you crazy?' She grabbed his jacket. 'He could be anywhere.'

'I know.'

'Why are you moving, then?'

'We need to find a clearing.'

'Why?' If looks could kill, he would have been not only dead, but also charred.

'To set *our* trap.'

Chapter 63

Sara argued once more but kept quiet when Zeb held a finger up.

He resumed his slow progress, passing underneath vegetation where possible, rising and skirting larger growth.

Cesar was right. This place is unapproachable without making noise.

He was sure the cartel boss had heard their arrival.

He will wait, however. He won't come after us.

He is down to three men. He can't risk more losses.

There was one spot that looked likely.

About fifteen square feet. Firs and ponderosas surrounding it.

He surveyed it critically. Looked around.

Nope.

Started crawling.

Didn't miss her eye roll.

Stifled a grin, and continued.

He found a better location at the far end of the pond, almost opposite to where they had arrived.

An open space similarly sized to the first.

In shadow, under the canopy of tall trees.

Dead leaves and sticks under their feet.

There were several fallen trees just beyond, and the pond was a five-minute walk away.

He shouldered the HK and inspected the logs.

A few were too large for his purpose, but there was a smaller one, half-buried in the earth.

He heaved at it and motioned the girl to stay back when she came forward to help.

'Keep watch.'

She watched, the AK in her hand, her eyes alternating between him and their surroundings.

'I have never fired a weapon.'

'They don't know that.'

'He could come any minute.'

'Nope. He will be wondering what we are doing. He will see if he can outwait us.'

He rolled the log to the center of the clearing.

Removed the length of rope from the backpack and looked up.

She gasped when she got his intent.

'You're—'

'Yeah.'

He fastened the length to the fallen tree and tossed the free end to her.

'Climb.'

Zeb was making a small fire when heard a twig crack.

He dived away, whirling, drawing his Glock, when two men came into the clearing.

Both carried AKs. Both weapons were pointed at him.

'Try it. You will die,' one of them barked.

He's right.

'At last,' Joachim Tavez stepped out from behind them.

He rubbed his hands and looked Zeb up and down.

'Who are you, gringo?' he asked, as Zeb got to his feet and tossed his handgun to the ground.

'The others, too,' Tavez warned him.

Zeb considered his options.

The cartel men were well spread out.

Sara was behind him, to his left, at the edge of the clearing.

He himself was at a side, under the shade of a giant tree.

'I won't kill you,' Tavez promised. There was no mirth in his eyes. They were flat, hard, and cold. 'Not right away.'

'You,' he turned to the girl. 'Get over here.'

She didn't move.

'You heard me?' He raised his voice.

'COME HERE.'

Sara fidgeted. Threw a scared look in Zeb's direction, but didn't leave her spot.

One of the shooters swore. He covered her with his weapon.

Strode forward impatiently.

Keeping well away from his fellow hitter's line of fire.

And tripped over the hidden rope.

Chapter 64

Zeb had whittled away a section of it until it held together by mere strands.

He had tied the free end, the one Sara had looped over a branch, to a rock in the center of the clearing and had buried it under leaves.

The threads snapped when the shooter fell over it.

The free end slipped across the leaves faster than a snake.

A rushing sound from above.

The hitter looked up.

Screamed as he saw the log heading right at him.

Zeb wasn't standing around to watch.

He dived for his Glock.

Got a hand around it.

His move roused the second shooter.

His AK chattered.

Someone yelled.

Sara shrieked.

Leaves flew around Zeb. Mud splattered him.

He rolled desperately. Got his weapon up.

Snapped two rounds.

Knew they missed.
Settled on his belly, momentarily.
Sight, barrel, and shooter came together for a fraction.
Trigger pull.
The gunman jerked.
Howled.
His AK drooped.
Zeb rolled once more.
Away from the girl, who was darting away into the forest.
Joachim Tavez's face was red. He was recovering. Shouting.
The shooter on the ground.
Slithering away as the log fell, missing him by mere inches.
The ground shaking and trembling momentarily.
Zeb rose to a crouch.
The fog swept over him.
Fired into shooter number two.
Dropped him.
Turned toward Joachim.
The cartel boss dived to the ground.
Clawing at his waist.
The first shooter was scrambling to his feet.
Zeb snapped a shot at Tavez.
And flew towards hitter number one.
An unexpected move that shocked the hitter, who froze.
Which was what Zeb wanted.
He body-slammed the killer.
Gritted his teeth when the AK crashed into his ribs.
Brought the Glock down on the man's face, savagely.
Turned him around just as Tavez fired.

Felt the killer stagger.

Whacked the man again.

Shot at Tavez, using the shooter's body as a shield.

Zeb missed.

The cartel boss didn't.

However, his rounds slammed into his man.

Zeb dived away from the falling shooter, triggering as fast as he could.

One of his rounds slammed into Tavez's shoulder, dropping him to the ground.

And then killer number two joined the fight.

He was propped up on his elbow.

His chest bloody.

His eyes raging.

His AK came up.

Zeb shot him, putting him down.

Turned rapidly around to the cartel boss.

The clearing was empty.

Joachim Tavez had escaped.

Chapter 65

Zeb could hear crashing in the forest.
Tavez should not get away.
'Tulip!' he roared, following the fleeing cartel boss.
'I am here,' Sara said, panting as she came from behind a thicket. 'I saw him. That way,' she pointed.
Away from the pond.
Toward the rocky slope.
Zeb grabbed her hand.
Reloaded his Glock instinctively.
And upped his pace.
Branches slapped their faces.
Agony raced through him.
Thigh.
He white-boxed the pain.
Stowed away the fury and the rage.
Summoned the calm.
Got his feet to roll on the ground.
Became a panther.
Breathed in and out, through the mouth.
Easily.

Making sure the girl was close behind him.

Ducking around trees, giving their trunks a wide berth to foil Tavez if he sprang out from behind one of them.

But the gang boss was easy to follow.

His panting and thrashing could be heard way ahead of them.

Zeb saw flashes of him.

Fifty yards away, running as fast as he could.

Zeb snapped a shot at him, more to slow Tavez down than to cause any injury.

The cartel man surprised him.

He stopped and took shelter behind a fir.

Fired a long burst at them.

'Gringo.'

Zeb heard him swear as he grabbed the girl and flung her to the ground, rounds peppering the air above them.

'I am not finished. I will still kill you. I will drink your blood.'

He laughed.

Zeb risked a look.

Tavez had resumed running.

Zeb got to his feet. Hauled Sara up.

Checked her swiftly for injuries.

Nothing apparent.

Continued the chase.

The trees started thinning out.

Joachim Tavez, knowing that he would be exposed soon, moved faster.

'Don't wait for me,' Sara gasped. 'Get after him.'

Zeb didn't.

Because protecting her was more important.

The distance between them and the gang boss widened.

They caught glimpses of him as he started ascending the slope.

Tavez was wily. Vicious. And smart.

That showed when he crouched behind a boulder.

And heaved it down at them.

The rock wasn't large.

Probably two or three feet in diameter.

However, it started gathering speed as it jumped and bounced alarmingly on the uneven surface.

Zeb and the girl lost precious seconds in getting out of its way.

By when, the distance between Tavez and them had widened to a hundred yards.

The cartel boss topped the rise.

Looked back at them.

Fired three rounds that whistled into the air and got lost in the open.

Tavez laughed, swore, and disappeared over the top.

Careful, Zeb warned himself.

He cut a wide loop to the left. They climbed carefully, as stealthily as they could, because they didn't know what lay beyond the rise.

Tavez could be lying in wait.

Zeb slowed as he neared the rise.

His Glock out, his eyes and ears alert.

His body shielding Sara.

He bent double and crossed the ridge in a flash.

Loose gravel. Round stones. Smooth slope.

Descending two hundred yards to a stream.

No sign of Tavez.
Zeb's foot slipped.
He started falling.
'Stay back,' he yelled at Sara as he lost his balance.
A shadow streaked across the slope.
'Watch out!'
Joachim Tavez pounced on him.

Chapter 66

Zeb turned just in time to block the descending knife.

He jabbed his left forearm up to stop Tavez's killing blow.

The Mexican was growling and swearing. A continual stream of words pouring out of his mouth, his eyes narrowed in concentration, and dark with hate.

He clubbed with his free hand, pounding Zeb on his face. On his neck. Wherever he could.

Fierce, punishing blows that shook Zeb to the core. He fell under the weight of the attack.

Started sliding.

Tavez on top of him. Lips parted, sweating pouring down on him. The knife arm still bearing down, Zeb still warding it off.

The cartel boss reared suddenly. He jammed his knee into the fallen man's thigh.

Zeb groaned aloud as his vision turned dark. The knee was crushing the bullet wound. Ripping open the slowly healing flesh.

He tried to heave off the attacker.

The Mexican laughed. He had found a weakness.

He yanked the knife hand away and plunged it straight at the thigh.

Zeb clawed, found a large stone, and clubbed it at his assailant.

Tavez jumped back. Zeb got to his feet shakily.

And collapsed when the gang boss lunged at him and brought him down.

The cartel leader was on his chest, pinning him down, his heels to each side of Zeb's body.

The rifles on his back slid smoothly on the loose gravel, like a lubricant.

The Mexican's blows were accelerating his descent.

Zeb stopped thinking when the knife headed to his eyes.

He smashed Tavez's neck.

The Mexican laughed.

The blade didn't waver. One inch away.

At the last minute, Zeb shoved with all his strength and turned his head away.

The knife struck rock. Metal clanged.

Tavez didn't pull away for another strike. He jabbed the hilt in Zeb's neck.

Right against a nerve.

Zeb yelled. Struck.

A glancing blow that caught the Mexican's nose. Split it. Blood started pouring down.

The gangster screamed.

He leaned back and struck with his knife.

Moved one knee to pin the operative's right hand.

The other leg to crash into the wounded thigh.

Zeb sucked air frantically. Trying to get oxygen to sweep away the blackness engulfing him.

Take the blow.

He steeled himself. Cried out when steel sank into his left shoulder.

Tavez was taken aback. He was expecting attack. Resistance.

For a fraction of a second his thrusting and pounding stopped.

Zeb roared. Jerked his legs up. Slammed his knees into the Mexican's back.

Tavez fell forward.

Zeb's right fist connected with his face.

A second blow smashed into the soft flesh just beneath the collarbone.

Tavez bellowed. Tried to release the knife for another thrust.

Zeb clamped his wrist. Squeezed with all his strength until the cartel man sobbed and released the knife.

But the Mexican didn't give up. He rained punishing blows on Zeb.

The operative retaliated, his right fist moving metronomically, landing on the man on top, wherever there was an opening.

A rib cracked.

Mine. The shrieking pain confirmed that.

His vision was fading.

But he didn't let up.

Brought up his left arm, even though it was bloody and weakened. Smashed it against Tavez's temple.

The killer fell away.

Zeb rolled on top.

Both men still sliding. Still heading to the bottom.

Someone screamed.

Sara.

He looked up.

They were accelerating.

Heading straight to large boulders jammed together.

With the last of his energy, he got both arms around Tavez's upper body.

Which buried the knife deeper inside him.

Ignore.

He hauled the Mexican up.

Kicked back with his legs.

To speed up their slide.

Crashed the killer's back against the rock.

A shriek escaped Tavez.

Zeb got a palm around his jaw.

The cartel man bit his fingers.

Ignore that too.

He slammed the killer's head against the stone.

Kept bashing it.

Till the screams turned to cries, to pleading.

No give. No mercy. No remorse.

Zeb pounded. The earth tilted. Blurred. He still continued, savagery possessing him.

Until his world turned dark.

Chapter 67

The sound of rushing water woke Zeb.

He lay motionless, memory returning.

Tavez. Sliding on rocks. Screaming. Yelling.

He blinked, trying to make out where he was.

Something soft beneath him.

He turned his head.

He was near the stream.

On the ground.

His jacket underneath him.

His shoulder almost numb with pain.

I took a knife.

He looked down. His T-shirt, what remained of it, was bloody. But the strapping on his wounds seemed to be new.

'I used Tavez's clothes.' Sara stood over him. Dark hollows under her eyes. Her fingers twisting. Clenching and unclenching.

'I didn't know if you would …' She swallowed.

Zeb tried to lift an arm. It felt heavy.

Darkness claimed him again.

The sun had set when he woke again.

He was lying where he had been earlier. Next to the flowing water.

Wisps of smoke assailed his nose.

He propped himself up slowly, gritting his teeth.

Sara was bent over a small fire. Holding a stick over it. Pieces of meat skewered on it.

Her smile, when she looked at him, was like the sun rising.

She helped him stand and took him to the water.

Stood by him as he bent and washed his face. Drank from the stream.

Cool, cool water that went inside.

Life.

'Thank you.'

She brushed his words away.

'You must be hungry.'

He was.

He bit into the pieces of meat. They were still raw. But he wouldn't trade them for the finest cuisine.

Strength returned. With it, awareness.

He got to his feet.

Tested his left leg and arm.

They felt like red-hot pokers were buried in them.

Deal with it.

He dealt with it in his usual way.

Went deep inside his mind.

To the white drawers that were rarely opened.

Many of them contained memories. Of laughter, blue eyes, and dimpled cheeks.

He opened an empty one.

Swept the agony into it and slid the drawer back.

And returned to the present.

'Where is he?'

'There. Behind the rocks. I dragged him away when you were out. Removed his clothing for your dressing.'

Her voice was matter-of-fact.

I have lived an adult life. He recollected her words.

He inspected his weapons. The HKs and the M24 had survived the fight with Tavez. They were badly scratched and their stocks had a couple of dents, but they were serviceable.

His Glocks and knives were intact.

I had no time to draw any weapon. He was on me so fast.

He stripped and started cleaning them.

'We head home tomorrow, ma'am.'

'Dad. I would like to find his …'

'I will come back, ma'am. Once you are safe.'

'You can hardly walk. You need to see a doctor.'

'I have been injured worse. The next campers we come across, we'll take their help.

'What about Namir?'

'He will have to wait.'

'If he doesn't?'

'Then he can meet Tavez.'

Chapter 68

'Did your father say anything about Namir? He did an investigative piece on him, didn't he?'

It was eight am on Saturday. A clear day, promising to be sunny and warm. A good sleep behind them. No further attacks. There were no more cartel killers left.

No sign of the terrorists.

Sara nodded, wisps of steam surrounding her face as she sipped the coffee Zeb had brewed.

He was feeling better. His injured limbs hindered movement and throbbed continually.

I am alive. That alone matters.

'It was a long time back.' She scrunched her face. 'Dad said he was the most brutal terrorist he had known of.'

'How so?'

'Namir likes killing. He has blood lust. I saw that with my own eyes.'

She shivered, her eyes clouding. 'But something else drives him. I remember Dad saying something. It will come to me.'

The stream was easy to cross. It was shallow, rocky,

making it a little more difficult for Zeb, but they got across it without much trouble.

The ascent over its bank had him gasping and sweating, and once on top, they took a breather.

'I was hoping to reach Erilyn this evening.'

'We won't, will we?'

'I don't think so, ma'am.'

They came across campers just after lunch.

They had covered thirty miles, not encountering another person.

At one point they had come across a black bear and her cubs.

Sara wanted to get closer to them, but Zeb pulled her back.

'It's their land,' he said, suppressing a grin at her mutinous expression. 'Besides, going to your grandfather is priority.'

Two miles away from the bears, they sniffed the distinctive odor.

Zeb dropped to the ground. She followed.

A slow crawl, senses alert.

Taking care not to rustle any bushes, until they spotted the tents.

Two of them, green, in front of a bunch of firs.

What was on the ground held his attention.

She gasped, turned away, and retched in the bushes.

Two bodies. Adults.

One male, one female.

Zeb's Glock was in his hand the moment she had thrown up.

The sound would have given away their presence.

No hostiles emerged, however.

The forest was quiet, except for their breathing and her soft crying.

He gestured at her to stay where she was and approached the camp cautiously.

The bodies bore marks of a struggle. Bruised faces and hands.

Both had died of knife wounds. Multiple stabs.

Someone likes killing, he thought bleakly.

He bit back an oath and tightened his lips when his eyes swept across the woman.

He hadn't noticed from the distance, but now, it was clear. She had been raped.

Her jeans were around her knees. Her privates exposed.

He heard the girl moving and blocked her immediately.

'You shouldn't see this.'

'Zeb, I grew up in Mosul. There is nothing that I haven't seen,' she sounded confident, but he detected the tremble.

She shoved past him and immediately fell to her knees, dry-heaving.

'Who could have done this?' she whispered.

Her hand flew to her mouth in horror when he replied.

'Namir.'

Chapter 69

Zeb shifted the bodies to inside one tent. It was bare. No possessions, no backpacks, no cellphones.

The other was in a similar state.

Why would Namir steal as well?

Supplies, he answered himself.

He hustled Sara out of the camp after making note of its location.

'Can you …?' she swallowed, 'How long ago do you think they were …?'

'Several hours, ma'am. Maybe sometime in the night. Not recently, for sure.'

He tried to work out just how much of a lead Namir had on them, and then gave up.

At least a day, if not more. We got sidetracked by Tavez. Lost time because of my wounds.

There was urgency now. Both of them striding swiftly. Wanting to catch up with the terrorists before they reached the town.

Or at least get to Erilyn as quickly as we can.

By late evening, their pace had slowed, however.

His thigh and shoulder were flaring up. His trouser leg had turned dark with blood, while his chest was wet.

They no longer had any loose clothing from which to fashion dressings.

He unbound the existing bandages, squeezed them and applied them again.

'It will have to do.'

'Let's walk through the night.'

'Let's not,' he countered. 'Namir isn't a fool. He could have posted watchers. We won't see them in the dark. Until it's too late.'

She didn't argue. He could see she was exhausted as well. Her shoulders drooped, her hair was matted to her forehead.

They made camp behind rocks, in an open plain, under the sky.

Cold rations and water to fill them up.

Stars and the thin sliver of the moon looking down at them.

'Churches,' she roused him as he was drifting into sleep.

'Huh?'

'Namir has a thing about churches.' She propped herself up on her elbow. 'It came to me. That time in Beirut. He had fired into a church. Dad said it wasn't the first time he attacked such places. There were other instances.'

Zeb examined it in his mind.

He didn't come all the way to this country just to kill Kenton Ashland.

However, he wasn't convinced of the church angle.

He settled back and stifled a yawn. 'Tomorrow. Let's deal with it then.'

He woke her at three am on Sunday.

'I thought you didn't want to travel in the night,' she grumped.

'It's the morning, ma'am.'

She snorted but followed him without a word.

They made good time in the cool of the dawning day.

He could sense her feelings as they neared the town.

Relief. Worry. Uncertainty.

'That couple.'

He cocked his head, waiting for her to continue.

'You put them inside their tent. There was no one for Dad. I fled.' Her voice broke.

'Ma'am,' He caught her shoulder and turned her around. 'I made you a promise. I'll hand you over to your grandfather and return. Kenton Ashland was a hero. He will have a hero's funeral.'

'My life, it's no more,' she sniffed.

He knew what she meant.

He hugged her as she broke down. Bawling and crying, wetting his shirt with her tears.

The weight of the last few days breaking her.

'I'm sorry,' she said, struggling to be free.

He released her.

'I tried to be strong. But …'

She sniffled and brushed her tears angrily.

She's only fifteen.

'Ma'am, crying isn't weakness.' He cursed himself for not finding better words. 'Your world has collapsed. It's normal to feel that life is dark. That there is no light.'

'I don't know what to do.'

'Your grandfather will. I will stay in town until we sort everything out. I will help him.'

'You will? Why? You have your own life. Work.' She half-laughed through her tears.

'Because if I didn't help, I couldn't look myself in the mirror.'

She looked at him for a long time. A teenager with tears on her cheeks, hair ruffling in the breeze, eyes large.

She looked at him while the Earth rotated on its axis and hurtled along its orbit.

Then she nodded, clasped his hand once and turned around.

Started walking toward Erilyn.

Which they reached at six am.

Chapter 70

Zeb kept them away from major streets and roads. They cut across office buildings and parking lots, all empty. It was early Sunday morning.

There was no traffic. No vehicles, no pedestrians.

Red lights blinked lazily at crossings.

'Gramps is on Farloe Street,' she spoke over his shoulder as they surveyed Main Street from the shelter of a bar's building.

'I know where it is.' She tugged at his jacket impatiently. 'Let's go.'

'Wait.'

He kept watching. Trying to get a feel for Erilyn.

It was like thousands of small towns across the country.

Main Street. Small stores. Banks. Wide pavements. Trees lining the sidewalks.

In the distance, the white spire of a church.

'What are you looking for?'

'Namir and his men.'

'You think he will be in town?'

'I don't know.'

He started again, taking his cues from her whispered directions.

She took the lead after a while, almost running in her haste to meet her grandfather.

'There.' She pointed to a white-walled house.

A large porch. A neatly maintained front yard. A pick-up truck in the driveway. A flag flapping in the wind.

It was the cruiser that drew his attention.

It was parked behind the truck. No one inside it.

Sara didn't heed his *wait up*.

She broke away from him, raced to the door and banged on it.

'Gramps!' she cried out.

She pounded it again, her tear-streaked face turning back once in Zeb's direction.

She had raised her fist again when the door opened.

A tall man opened the door.

White-haired. White shirt neatly tucked into blue jeans, despite the early hour.

Zeb climbed onto the porch.

The man didn't look at him. Worry lining his face.

Relief replacing it instantly.

'Honey,' he opened his hands.

Sara hugged him tight, sobbing.

The door shut behind them.

Zeb waited patiently. He could hear the crying from inside. Muffled questions. Broken answers.

The old man's 'My God!'

Another voice joined in.

Rapid footsteps approached the door.

It opened again.

Sara, brushing her eyes with her sleeve.

'Sorry, Zeb. Please come in. Gramps, this is—'

'Mr. Carter?' A burly police officer brushed past the girl. 'Chief of Police Terry Schwartz.'

The porch steps creaked.

A uniformed deputy was climbing up the steps behind him, not in the best of shape. Huffing, wheezing. *Reid Frazier*, his nameplate proclaimed. 'You got licenses for those guns, buddy?'

'You're carrying many injuries, Mr. Carter.' Schwartz stated, his face expressionless, his hands close to his holstered gun.

'The HKs, the M24, those aren't mine. I've got permits for the Glocks,' Zeb replied. 'The wounds … we met some people.'

Something's not right.

'Can I see them? The licenses?' Frazier extended a hand, barely concealing a knowing look. His free arm was hooked on his belt.

'Not here, Reid. Sara and Pete have a lot of talking to do.'

'Pete?' he called over his shoulder, his eyes still on Zeb.

'Yes?' the grandfather's face was wrinkled with worry, hugging the girl with one hand.

'I'll send over an ambulance. Another cruiser, but that might take a while. We're short-handed, as you know.'

The white-haired man nodded, his eyes meeting Zeb's briefly. Dropping away.

He's embarrassed?

'Mr. Carter. You need to come along with us, sir. Hand over your weapons. Slowly.'

'What?' Sara exclaimed, freeing herself and pushing

forward, as the cops took his guns. 'No. Zeb helped me. Gramps, what's going on?'

'They are taking him to the station, honey. To answer some questions. It's routine.'

'No!' She grabbed Frazier by the shoulder and spun him around. 'He saved my life.'

'That's not the story we heard, ma'am.'

A shocked silence.

'What?' she breathed.

'We have witnesses. Mr. Carter killed some hikers. He might have been involved in Kenton's death.'

Chapter 71

'That's a lie,' Sara cried out. 'Namir killed dad. I was there. I escaped. Came across Zeb's camp. He protected me from those terrorists. He didn't kill any hikers.'

'That's not the eyewitness statement we have. We'll get to the bottom of it in any case. Pete?'

The grandfather tugged at the girl's hand, drawing her away. 'Terry will sort it out, honey.'

'No,' she yelled, her face turning red. 'It's not right. It's not true.'

'Ma'am?' Zeb addressed her, 'It's all right. I will go with them.'

'But you didn't—' Her lips trembled. Tears coursed down her face.

'I know. But it's not a big deal. Just some questions.'

Frazier jerked his head at the cruiser. Stomped off. Zeb followed, Schwartz covering from behind.

Frazier opened the door for him and pushed him inside with a shove.

He was grinning. A savage killer was in his custody.

Couldn't help sniggering at how easily they had captured

Zeb. Slid behind the wheel and chuckled at Schwartz, next to him.

Zeb saw the girl's face at a window. Pale, blurred. Then they turned a corner.

'These hikers I am supposed—'

The deputy pulled into a parking space and slammed the brake.

'Not supposed to,' he said, viciously, as he turned around. 'Here.' He fumbled in a pocket and brought out his cell.

He thumbed at it and played a video. A man speaking nervously, blood on his face.

'This dude came from nowhere. Pointed a gun at us. Roughed Jake up. Killed him and my friends. There was a girl with him.'

'Frazier, that's enough. Let's get to the station.' Schwartz was edgy, uneasy. Worried that his officer would mishandle the biggest arrest of their lives.

Zeb ignored the byplay.

That's Chuck. That drunk hiker.

'How did you get that video? Chuck walked in?'

'No,' the deputy gloated. 'It was handed to us.'

'By whom?'

'Another witness. You're done, buddy,' he chortled. 'We have witnesses coming out of our ears.'

'This witness has a name?'

'Sure as hell he does,' Frazier started the cruiser and pulled out. 'He came last night. With this video. Told us everything about you. The chief sent some officers into the wilderness. To bring back the bodies.'

He met Zeb's eyes in the mirror and smirked, 'You walked right up to us. Talk about being stupid!'

'Frazier, shut your lips and drive,' Schwartz commanded.
'This witness?' Zeb tried again.
'A Canadian businessman. John Leopard.'

Chapter 72

Zeb fell back as if punched.

Leopard. That's Namir.

He stared out blindly as the cruiser sped on the quiet streets.

He must have forced Chuck to make that video. After killing Jake and the others.

Chuck's probably dead, too.

Fed some story to Schwartz and Frazier that I killed Ashland. And made off with Sara.

Why did they buy it?

The two officers were conferring quietly in the front.

Small-town cops. Drunks, petty thefts are all they have handled.

Zeb could see how it might have gone.

Namir walks in, probably with his face bruised, signs of escape. Comes up with a story and video.

Why wouldn't they believe him?

What's the terrorist's angle? He'll know his story won't wash. Eventually.

Another urgent thought entered his mind.

Clare needs to know.

Tires squealed as Frazier Nascar-ed the vehicle through a turn and brought it up to a shuddering stop in front of a yellow, squat building: the police station.

Schwartz stepped out and came around to Zeb's door, which was opened by the deputy.

Zeb struck.

He kicked the door as Frazier was opening it.

Thankful that he wasn't cuffed.

Metal crashed into the deputy.

He howled and bent over, clutching his face.

Zeb sprang out.

Schwartz swore, his hand darting to his gun.

Zeb body-shoved Frazier at him, and the two men collided.

Ample flesh met a large mass.

Someone grunted. A string of curses as both men fell.

Zeb took off.

He ran in the direction of the wilderness, the route he and the girl had taken when entering town.

Heard shouting behind him.

A wild shot that smashed into a store window.

He threw himself into an alley just as another round chipped concrete.

Need a cellphone.

The alley was a dead-end. Trash cans lining its end. A boarded wall blocking it.

He leaped on top of a can. Right leg to lever himself up, right arm grabbing the top and pulling himself over.

A small yard. Leading to a park.

He cut around the park, heading back. Toward Pete Ashland's house.

RUN!

They won't expect me to head there.

A dog walker approached in the distance.

Won't be good if he spots my bloodied jacket and thigh.

Zeb leaped over a fence, into a back garden, down a narrow path, over a gate and back onto a street.

This runs parallel to Main Street, he visualized.

Not far from Farloe Street.

He slowed to a walk. Head bent down. Hands in pockets.

Turned into the grandfather's street.

There were several parked cars. But no cruiser.

The pickup was still in the driveway.

No faces at windows.

He drifted to the side of the house, ducking through a hedge that separated the property from the neighbor's.

And came to a wooden fence that surrounded the yard.

It was as tall as he was and required a few attempts to scale.

A stone path in a green lawn, leading to a glass door.

He tried it.

It opened without a sound.

He entered the warmth of the house.

Utility room. Washer. Laundry drying.

He went to the door and entered the dining room.

Seated himself at the empty table and was pouring himself a glass of water when Sara Ashland entered the room.

'Zeb!'

Chapter 73

A muffled voice came from inside the house.

Pete Ashland rushed into the room, a shotgun in his hand, trained squarely on the intruder.

Zeb emptied the glass and placed it back.

'Sir, I didn't kill your son. Or any of those campers.'

Blue eyes pinning him down. Unwavering. Examining him. The weapon not moving an inch.

One of those salt-of-the-earth kind of men, Zeb decided.

He didn't say any more, letting the grandfather make his mind up.

A refrigerator hummed somewhere, a clock ticked.

And then Ashland moved.

He lowered the shotgun and placed it on the table.

'I am sorry, Mr. Carter,' he replied formally. 'Sara told me everything. Once the cops had gone. I was planning to come to the station. See what was happening. Bail you out if necessary.'

'They released you?' the girl couldn't contain herself.

'I released myself.'

'Well,' Pete Ashland fingered his beard, his eyes crinkling.

'Looks like you'll definitely need my help.'

Zeb forestalled any more questions. 'Sir, I need a phone.'

'Yes.' He didn't ask why. Dug into his pocket and withdrew one.

He sent a text message to a number.

Isambard.

The message let the recipient know that he was using an unsecure phone. And that there were civilians around.

The cell rang promptly.

'Where are you? What happened?'

Clare, his boss, didn't beat about the bush. She didn't waste time on pleasantries. There would be time for questions. Such as why his sat phone had gone off the radar. Why his GPS trackers weren't online.

Now wasn't the time.

'Erilyn, ma'am.'

He heard her fingers click.

'Idaho?'

'Yes, ma'am.'

'What's the problem?'

'Namir is here.'

He heard an indrawn breath. She listened without interruption as he briefed her rapidly. He didn't tell her about Joachim Tavez.

That, too, could wait.

He could feel Ashland and Sara's eyes on him. Questions on their faces. Amazement. Worry.

'Our team is scattered. I'll organize SWAT. State police. I'll get back to you.'

'One more favor, ma'am.'

'Ask.'

'Pete Ashland,' he smiled slightly when the grandfather's bushy eyebrows twitched. 'He still has some doubts.'

'Give him the phone.'

'My boss,' Zeb explained and handed the cell over.

'Hello?' Ashland spoke uncertainly.

He turned sideways, looking at the back yard, hugging Sara as she tried to overhear.

'You are, ma'am?'

'The president, ma'am?' His voice rose.

He stood straight. Meeting the girl's eyes when her mouth rounded in an O.

'No, ma'am. That won't be necessary. I am sure he's a busy man.'

'Yes, ma'am,' he replied drily, this time looking over Zeb. 'He's bleeding. Shoulder. Thigh. But he seems to be functioning.'

'Yes, ma'am. I can see that. Thank you, ma'am. It is an honor.'

He ended the call and pocketed his cell.

His eyes were still wondering.

'She said she could get the president to call me. If I still needed convincing. She can do that?'

'Yeah.'

'How can I help?'

A siren wailed as a cruiser rolled up the driveway.

Zeb thumbed towards the front of the house.

'With that, for starters.'

Chapter 74

'For Christ's sake, Terry! You got to wake the neighborhood?' Zeb heard Ashland growling at the visitors. 'What happened to your face?'

The police chief replied indistinctly.

'He escaped? How?' The grandfather, astonished.

More mumbled responses.

'Well, he's not here. Don't stand there, jawing. Find him. Beats me how the heck he could get away from you.'

He slammed the door shut and returned, rubbing his hands in glee.

'He's gone. I've got to admit, I enjoyed that.'

'What did he tell you about Namir? This dude, Leopard?'

Ashland put the coffee pot to boil. 'Not much. That he turned up at night. With a few other men. Had this video. Told us his story. That he found my son dead. He sent several deputies to the wilderness. In the night. To bring back his body.'

For a few moments, his shoulders stooped. His age showed.

He poured the brew into three cups and handed them out.

'What was he doing in the wilderness? Leopard.'

'Camping.'

'Why didn't the chief believe Sara?'

'Terry's got a big ego. Thinks a lot of himself,' Ashland grimaced. 'Is easily impressed by fancy clothes and words. *Stockholm syndrome*, he said, when she wasn't listening.'

Sara swore, looked apologetic when her grandfather looked sternly at her.

'Where's Leopard staying?'

'The Downtown Hotel.' He pointed toward Main Street. 'That's really a hotel.'

Why would Namir still be hanging around? Why wouldn't he flee to the Canadian border?

Zeb closed his eyes when the coffee went down in him.

Strong, bitter, bringing every sense alive.

A bell tolled in the distance.

Another sip.

Bell.

Something about it.

He pored through his memory, trying to pin down the elusive thought.

Sara was talking to Ashland, her voice breaking.

Zeb not paying attention. Just hearing the occasional word.

'Dad … Sunday Service … back in time.'

Church.

What about it?

Namir has a thing about churches.

The chair clattered back when Zeb rose in a flash.

'The church. What time is the service?'

Ashland gaped at him for a moment.

'Eight,' he said, recovering under Zeb's intense gaze.

'How many go to it?'

'About fifty. But today's special. The high school choir is singing. We're expecting double.'

'Of course.' Sara cupped her hand to her mouth.

'It's Beirut again. He will kill them.'

Chapter 75

Zeb reached out silently for Ashland's phone.

'Ma'am, Namir will attack the church.' He glanced at a wall clock.

Seven thirty-five am.

'At eight. Hold up a second. Does it start exactly on time?' he fired at Ashland.

'No,' the grandfather replied quickly, 'eight-fifteen is when it starts. That's when everyone arrives. However, before that, there's choir. Singing. Actual service is when everyone comes. Eight-fifteen.'

'Eight-fifteen, ma'am.'

'This is Namir. He will fire then. For maximum impact. He would have done his homework.'

'Agreed, ma'am.'

'SWAT's at least forty-five minutes away. The State Police, too. They are dealing with several unrelated incidents. What about local police?'

'Incompetent, ma'am. And just …'

'Two of them,' Ashland completed for him. 'The rest have gone into the forest.'

'You heard, ma'am.' A thought struck him. 'There's something you can do. Call Terry Schwartz. He's the chief. Drill some sense into him.'

'Yes. He has to call Namir and tell him you are in custody?'

'Yes, ma'am. And then go about his business as normal. Stay away from the church. No sirens. No fast moves. That might trigger the killing.'

'You are going in?'

'Yes, ma'am.'

'Your sat phone? Vest?'

'Nothing, ma'am.'

She didn't dissuade him.

'Carry a cell.'

'I'll have Ashland's with me.'

'Forty-five minutes, Zeb. You need to stall them for that much time. Whatever it takes.'

'Yes, ma'am.'

A hundred people could be dead in that interval. He didn't say that. Clare knew. Just like she knew stalling wouldn't be his strategy.

'Sir, the church's layout? Can you describe it?' he asked the white-haired man when he had hung up.

'I can do better,' Ashland grabbed a sheet of paper, a pencil, and drew swiftly.

Strong, straight lines. Shadowing for walls.

'Main doors,' he pointed to the front of the church.

'Parking to the sides.

The church was a simple long rectangle, the short ends at the front and the back.

'A rear exit. More parking there.'

'Gramps, the side entrance,' Sara prompted.

'Yes. Nearly forgot that.' He drew a small door on the right side, while the girl scurried to a drawer and brought out a key on a chain.

'That's to the staircase that goes to the balcony. An outside entrance. You can enter the church that way, too. It's hardly used. Most people think it's boarded up. It's like a secret exit. People can go up or down, or in and out. There's inside access to the balcony, too. Which is how everyone climbs up. We have a key. A few other families have one.'

He tapped the sheet and raised his head. 'Not many people know of it. Maybe, just maybe, this terrorist doesn't, either.'

The elevated section was at the front of the church. Looking down on the pews and facing the altar.

'Hanging lights from the ceiling. Several of them. Two smaller balconies. One on each side. No real access to them. The first one was erected by mistake. The other … well, that went in just to complement.'

The smaller elevations were at the same height as the larger balcony.

'Wooden rails.'

'Anything else?'

'Confession booth to one side. A small room behind the altar. Access from the rear, as well as from the inside of the church. Nothing else.'

'What are the opening times?'

Ashland looked up quickly.

'This is a small town, Zeb. The church never shuts.'

'You got any weapons, sir? Not the shotgun.'

'Thought you'd never ask.'

Ashland went to an inner room and returned with a Sig Sauer and several mags. A wicked-looking knife as well.

'Kenton's,' he indicated at the gun. 'He kept a spare here. For self-defense.'

'Sir, is there anyone you can call? Warn?'

'That's the problem, Zeb. The church. It is in a dead zone. No signal.'

'Call your neighbors. Friends. But be careful. If Namir suspects something, he'll start shooting.'

'They should act like nothing's happening? But stay away from church?'

'Exactly.'

'I'll come with you. Sara can make the calls.'

'No, sir. You need to be here. With her.'

Because she's the sole witness to her father's murder.

Chapter 76

Zeb took Ashland's Ford pickup. Borrowed his jacket to change his appearance.

A Bass Pro cap on his head.

He drove in the direction of the church, keeping a lookout for Schwartz or any cruiser.

He had one Sig and six mags.

And was going up against ten terrorists.

The balcony. That's where most of Namir's men will be. It will give them the firing angle.

Some at the front and rear entrance. To finish the job.

The building came into view.

Men and women, families, hurrying inside, all of them dressed formally.

The choir was easy to spot.

Bright-eyed girls and boys. Neatly turned out. Walking in a group.

Zeb didn't spot any Middle-Eastern looking men.

He wasn't looking hard.

He drove past the church and parked in the driveway of an empty-looking house.

Walked back casually, hands in his pockets, trying not to let his limp show.

I won't be doing any running.
Only killing.
Or dying.

He walked past the church, cut a wide loop, and returned.

By then, there was hardly anyone outside.

A family hurried inside and the doors shut behind them.

They'll have getaway vehicles. Namir is not a suicide bomber.

Zeb scanned the parked cars and trucks in the front. All of them empty. No engines running.

May not be here. Too obvious.

He pulled his cell out.

Made a show of speaking to an imaginary caller, while he walked the length of the church.

Noted the side entrance Sara had pointed out: a wooden door, set flush in the concrete wall.

The first car came into view.

A Ford.

Then a Dodge. A Toyota. Another Toyota.

He paused, as if listening to his caller.

And heard a running engine.

He turned around slowly.

The vehicle wasn't visible.

He dropped beneath the window line of the Ford and moved swiftly down the line.

Until he spotted fumes coming out of an exhaust.

A black SUV.

Darkened windows.

Facing out.

For a quick getaway.

Why just one vehicle? Namir has nine more men. There should be one more.

Fear gripped him for a moment. That he had been spotted by the second vehicle.

He remained in a crouch. Scanning.

And gradually relaxed.

There was just the one SUV that had its engine running. All the other vehicles were empty.

Maybe the other one's parked somewhere down the street. Now to check if the SUV's occupant is Namir's man.

Chapter 77

Zeb looked around on the ground.

There, that was a cigarette stub. It would do.

He picked it up, wiped it, and put it in his mouth.

Stepped out from behind the vehicles, his phone held to his ear, patting his pockets.

A smoker searching for a light.

He strolled down the length of the parking lot, and when he saw the driver in the SUV, stopped.

Approached, still talking, still searching for a flame.

Knocked on the SUV's window.

It rolled down.

Dark hair. Dark beard. Black eyes.

Could still mean nothing.

He could be a highly respected community member.

'Where's Abbas?' Zeb asked irritatedly, in Arabic.

'Abbas?' The man's brows drew together in astonishment. 'He's dea–'

Realization flooded through him.

His hand snaked towards the empty seat.

Started bringing up an HK.

Stopped abruptly.

Because Zeb's Sig had crashed into his mouth, broken a couple of teeth and was jammed tight.

'Where are the others?'

The killer's eyes were wide. A thin sheen of sweat appeared on his forehead.

He swallowed audibly.

His hand twitched on his weapon.

'Where are they?' Zeb snarled.

His finger tightened on the trigger.

The killer moaned, but still didn't speak.

Zeb moved in a flash.

Still pressing the barrel against him, his left hand darted.

Grabbed the blade.

Sank it into the terrorist's shoulder.

Withdrew the gun.

Smashed the barrel against his throat.

The killer's scream choked away.

He doubled over. Heaving. Retching. Tears streaming down his face.

His HK forgotten.

Zeb pulled out the knife. Sheathed it in one motion.

Grabbed his hair. Yanked him upright.

'Last chance. And I hope you don't answer. I hope you shout. Or yell. Or beg.'

He smiled menacingly when the shooter looked at him uncomprehendingly, still in shock.

'Because I know what you were planning to do to the girl.'

'Five. Inside,' the killer's hands rose in pleading.

'Namir?'

'Sayidi not inside.'

'Where is he?'

'Nooo,' he moaned when Zeb twisted the barrel into his shoulder. 'Don't know. I swear. Only five.'

'Why?'

Broken sentences came out from his mouth.

Zeb put them together.

They were to start firing at eight-thirty am. No agreed signal. Just shoot at that time.

Then rush out.

The driver would bring the vehicle to the front.

They would climb in.

And get away.

'What about Namir?'

'Sayidi said he will join us.'

'Where?'

'Don't know,' the terrorist groaned. 'I told you.'

'Not Namir. The five men.'

The killer told him where they were located in the church.

'What's your name?'

'Why?' The terrorist tried to be defiant.

Zeb slapped him hard.

'Tell me.'

'Tahir.'

After which Zeb slashed his neck.

Chapter 78

Two men just inside the front entrance.

Three on the balcony.

No cellphone contact.

Zeb searched Tahir's body swiftly.

Ashland said service starts at eight-fifteen. But Tahir said shooting time was eight-thirty. His window of action had widened fractionally.

He found the fake Saudi identity document they all were carrying. He pocketed it and continued searching.

He found a cellphone.

Basic black. Like the one Abbas had.

He pondered where Namir and the three other killers were. And why they weren't in the church, or near it.

Then stopped thinking about them.

Because the clock was ticking.

He grabbed the killer's HK.

Nope. It will be visible.

He tossed it back into the SUV.

Took its keys and slashed its tires.

Show time.

Ashland had warned him away from using the rear entrance because, while it was concealed by a passage, there was no way to slip inside without the congregation noticing.

He loped to the side door.

The key fit easily.

He prayed it wouldn't make any noise.

It did.

It creaked.

He froze.

But then realized that the choir was singing. The congregation, too.

No one would hear the door opening.

He slipped inside and shut it behind him, suddenly enveloped in darkness because the door was covered by a thick curtain that blocked out all light.

He waited for his eyes to adjust.

He was in a narrow alcove.

Curtained.

To his left were steps.

Going up to the balcony, as Ashland had said.

In front of him was heavy fabric.

He knelt to the floor, wincing when the wound in his thigh shot bolts of fire.

Ignore.

He put his cheek to the floor and raised the curtain's hem.

The nearest row of benches was ten feet away.

Well-shod feet met his eyes.

Men in suits. Women in dresses. Children. All singing. All looking straight ahead.

The curtain ran the length of the church.

No one noticed him.

He tried to look up at the balcony, but the angle was inconvenient.

He let the fabric drop and stood.

The two men. They're probably at the corners at the rear.

He thought of stepping out and heading to the back, wearing a shame-faced expression. Like a latecomer.

The shooters on the balcony could spot me.

He decided to crawl, using the curtain as cover.

Seven-fifty am.

Chapter 79

It was slow going. Every five steps he stopped to look out cautiously. Saw nothing other than the legs of the churchgoers.

No one whispered, shouted, or shot at him.

Midway, he paused. Flexed his hands. Fingered the Sig.

And set off again.

And bumped his head against the corner.

His blood turned cold.

Reached faster than I expected.

The killer could be here.

Time slowed as he lifted the curtain a fraction of an inch at a time.

Didn't see any feet for a moment.

The rows of people started thirty feet away from the front entrance.

That side of the rectangle was about sixty feet wide, the large wooden doors right in the center.

He felt movement before he saw it.

Dust rising from the ground.

A pair of shoes moved.

Sneakers, not black shoes like the rest.

Twelve feet away. Pointing to the altar.

He rose to his feet, moving each muscle as slowly and carefully as he could.

Not disturbing the curtain.

And then risked a glance around its edge.

The fabric covered the shorter wall, too. The heavy drapery, dark red, hung from twenty feet and ran all around the interior surfaces. Above it were windows and lighting.

A bearded man was in his line of sight, wearing sneakers instead of the polished shoes everyone else wore. A shirt tucked into a pair of jeans.

Looking ahead.

Both hands behind his back.

Clasping an HK.

Zeb looked beyond the man, to the far end.

No shooter in sight.

Raised his eyes.

Spotted the small balcony high above, to the left of the altar.

That's not the big one. That's the one built by mistake.

There was a window in the balcony, light streaming from it, making it difficult for him to see into it.

He turned his attention back to the killer.

No Sig. The sound will carry. Cause everyone to fire.

He put the gun in his waist.

Drew the hunting knife out with his right hand.

Concealed it against his thigh.

And stepped out from behind the curtain.

Looking at the altar, moving his lips.

The choir not visible. Hidden by the standing congregation.

The giant crucifix drawing everyone's attention. Candles

lit all over the place.

Saw the terrorist glance sharply at him.

Felt his gaze assessing him.

Two more steps.

Looked directly at the man.

Made an apologetic face.

Bathroom, he mouthed.

The killer's face was still suspicious. His stance changed to face Zeb. Hands still behind his back.

No other killer in sight.

Two more paces.

Now, within an arm's length.

Zeb lunged as the killer started to move, his hands coming from behind.

The HK coming around.

His mouth opening to shout a warning.

The knife sank into the gunman's throat.

Zeb jabbed his forearm over the man's lips. Brought his struggling body to the ground.

Muffled the clank of the rifle with a thigh.

Held him down, looking up and around.

The disturbance hadn't caught anyone's attention.

No other killer in sight.

The body stilled.

He dragged it quickly behind the curtain.

Concealed it as well as he could.

Grabbed the killer's phone.

Looked at his watch.

Eight oh-five am.

Chapter 80

Zeb went behind the curtain again, after passing the double doors.

He fell to the ground and crawled swiftly toward the far wall.

Stopped abruptly when he felt footsteps.

Looked out cautiously from beneath the edge.

A pair of sneakers coming around the corner. Heading in his direction.

He's wondering where the killer is.

Zeb waited. A plan forming in his mind.

The terrorist quickened his pace.

He's not worried. Not just yet.

Fifteen feet away.

Twelve.

Eight.

Five.

Now!

Zeb sprang out.

Right hand yanking the killer's leg. Pulling hard.

Bringing him to the ground.

Left hand going around his back. Shielding his fall. To reduce the sound of impact.

Right hand flying to his mouth.

Grabbing the blade from between his teeth.

Plunging it into the neck.

Pressing an elbow into the face. Burying his sleeves in the man's mouth.

Covering the killer's body with his.

Lying there, but head up, eyes alert, looking around.

Luck favored him yet again.

Organ music had drowned out the sound of the scuffle.

He dumped the still trembling body in the corner. Pocketed the man's phone. Pulled the fabric in front of the body.

Ran down the length of the church again, using the cover of the drapery.

Hoping, praying, that no one had noticed the disturbance in the curtains.

Reached the side entrance unnoticed.

Took a minute to gather his breath.

Checked himself.

Blood trickling down his leg.

Not a new injury.

Left shoulder throbbing.

That, too, isn't new.

No scratch on him.

He had used surprise, stealth, and speed to his advantage.

He recalled the grandfather's sketch.

The top of the stairs opened into the balcony.

Ashland didn't mention any curtains. But then, he didn't speak of drapery at all.

Eight-fifteen am.

Zeb started climbing up, this time with the Sig in his hand. Because there was no more time for stealth.

Chapter 81

The steps were concrete, for which he was thankful.

Wooden steps would have creaked. Would have given me away.

Less than a minute to climb them. The singing drowning out every sound. Except his own breathing.

He could hear himself panting.

Knew he was in bad shape. His thigh was festering. His shoulder wasn't getting time to heal.

He stopped thinking when he reached the top.

A small, square opening. Concrete walls to one side, wood everywhere else.

The door was set flush in wood.

A rounded knob that was cold to his palm.

No one's handled it recently.

He fingered around it. Found a keyhole, and dropped to his knees.

He had a narrowed view through the opening.

Balcony stretching out ahead, well-lit by chandeliers high above.

No chairs.

Carpet on the floor.

One killer. Close, so close that if he opened the door, he could grab him.

Another killer ten or twelve feet away.

Both of them kneeling, peering through the posts of the wooden balustrade.

HKs or some kind of automatics in their hands.

Where's the third?

Zeb craned his head and angled it from side to side.

Nope. Just the two, as far as he could see.

The balcony wasn't large—twenty feet wide, and he could see a large part of it through the keyhole.

The door at its rear was visible, a dull-red *EXIT* sign glowing above it.

To one side were chairs, stacked on top of one another.

He could be outside that door.

Or just beside this keyhole. Where I can't see.

Eight-seventeen am.

No time to lose.

He stood up.

Froze when his knees clicked.

Brought the Sig up in a flash.

Stood to the side.

The door didn't crash open.

He didn't hear any movement from the other side.

Of course, he mentally slapped his forehead.

They can't hear above the voices of the congregation.

He bent and put his eye to the keyhole.

Just to be sure.

Let his breath out in a sigh of relief.

Get moving.

The clock's ticking.
He put his left hand to the door knob.
Twisted it lightly.
It turned.
He took a deep breath.
And yanked the door open.

Chapter 82

Zeb had planned to fire on the first shooter. And somehow get to the second. That part of his plan was hazy.

However, he ditched all his moves in an instant.

The killer in front of him was close, so close that shooting wasn't necessary.

The shooter was rooted to his spot. His head snapping around.

Taking in the new arrival.

Brain not comprehending what his eyes were seeing.

Zeb moved.

Thinking stopped.

Instinct, training, and experience took over.

His right hand rose.

Blurred down savagely, the Sig's barrel chopping the shooter on the side of his head.

A ferocious blow, with all his power and rage behind it.

His gun split the killer's skin.

The man fell without a sound.

His rifle followed.

No clatter.

Because the carpet was thick. Soft beneath Zeb's feet.

He wasn't stopping to watch, however.

Because the second killer was there.

He was recovering faster than the first.

Rising. Turning.

Zeb became motion. He became speed. His body became a weapon as he arrowed out.

Hurtling, closing the small distance between them.

His left shoulder crashing into the HK's rising barrel.

His right hand slashing at the killer's face.

His left hand punching him in the mouth.

Jabbing his fingers between his teeth.

Choking him.

Preventing him from making a sound.

Bringing the man down.

His gun rising up.

Falling down.

Crushing the killer's face.

Who wasn't giving up.

The shooter tried to heave his attacker away.

The gunman bit the invading fingers.

Zeb was only dimly aware of the biting pressure.

The rational part of his mind knew his digits had burst. Blood was spilling out of them.

That the slickness down his side was more blood seeping out of his shoulder.

Animal brain had taken over, however.

It chose fight over flight.

It fired orders.

Those signals jumped across from nerve to muscle.

Muscle contracted.

Zeb's hand came down in a blow.

It rose and fell.

More messages issued from animal brain.

Ignore the pounding from the man below.

Don't ignore that hand reaching for a knife.

Zeb thrust his bleeding fingers down the killer's throat.

Cutting off his air supply.

Brought the Sig down in a brutal arc.

The shooter gasped.

His eyes rolled in his head.

He groaned.

Zeb crushed his mouth.

And lay panting on top of him as the man stilled.

Chapter 83

Zeb took a few seconds to recover.

Looked between the wooden posts.

No heads turning his way.

Rolled to his knees. Got up and raced to the exit.

Put an ear to the door.

Placed a hand to the knob and opened the door suddenly.

Narrow passage. Well lit. Leading to stairs below.

No gunman.

Two dead on the ground floor. Two more down, in the balcony. Where's the fifth?

He whirled around.

Inspected the balcony quickly.

No place for any shooter to hide.

The walls were bare. Just the carpet extending from the rails to the rear.

The opposite wall had no doors.

No other human.

He darted to the balustrade and looked at the smaller alcove on the right.

It was twenty feet away, on the side wall.

It was at the same height as the balcony.

Bright light from a chandelier illuminating it.

It was nothing more than a narrow opening in the wall, protected by wooden rails, and had a small floor.

Built by mistake. That's what Ashland said. They later realized it had no access. Finished building it for show. Added the opposite one to complement it.

He turned to the one on the left.

Less light there.

But enough for him to see a dark shadow on its floor.

Zeb blinked the sweat away from his eyes.

Looked to one side of the balcony, allowing the shape to take form.

And turn into a man, lying prone.

A shooter.

Why didn't he spot me? See the fight?

The answer came to him in a flash.

Balcony lights would be in his eyes.

He didn't want to risk blind spots by looking this way.

If he moved, chances are he would be spotted by those below.

The gunman lay motionless. An occasional, barely perceptible movement of his head giving him away.

He stared down his HK's barrel, which jutted out an inch from the balcony.

Zeb reluctantly admired the tactics.

Lying down, no one can see him.

How do I get there, though?

Without warning him?

There were no steps to the narrow space.

Cleaners had to use ladders to get to it.

Too far for me to jump.

A line of lamps hanging from the ceiling extended down the center line of the church.

The lights were suspended thirty feet above the ground on twisted black cables, the nearest less than ten feet away from Zeb.

He considered it.

Looked at the shooter again.

Made his decision.

It was Tarzan time.

Chapter 84

Eight twenty-five am.

He ran through his options again.

There was no other way.

There was no more time.

He could try shooting the killer. But there was too much risk. Distance, lighting, angle, his own condition. There were too many factors against him.

He could warn the churchgoers. But that could set the shooter off.

Only one way.

He wiped his palms against his thighs.

Curled his right hand around the Sig.

Rose slowly, careful not to make sudden, sharp moves that could alert the shooter.

Went to the rear of the balcony.

Turned. Back to the wall. Face to altar.

Took a deep breath.

And ran.

Towards the balcony.

Six long steps away.

His left leg screaming, telling him it wasn't designed for heavy-duty work. Not after a round had gone through it.

Zeb didn't pay it any attention.

His body would heal.

Dead people wouldn't.

Three steps.

Two.

One.

He flew into the air, his right foot landing on top of the wooden railing.

Giving him the lift-off.

Flying through the air.

Right at the nearest hanging light.

His left hand reaching out.

Fingers spreading wide.

Someone moving to his left.

The shooter. His head bobbing as *he* sensed movement.

Zeb's palm curled around the thick cables.

His fingers slipped.

His shoulder felt wrenched out of its socket.

His left leg slapped against the wires.

It twisted around, the way a climber gripped rope.

His downslide slowed. Then stopped.

His own panting in his ears.

The momentum of his flight making the cable swing.

Carrying him across the church.

Bringing him across the shooter's balcony.

Where the killer was rising.

Getting to his knees.

Zeb's vision working like a camera.

Snapping images.

Beard. Brown hair. Mouth opening.

A few people below, sensing the disturbance.

Looking up.

Zeb still at an angle.

The shooter to his front and a few degrees to his right.

Zeb's Sig rising.

His left hand and leg gripping the cable tight.

Keeping him straight as a pillar.

The shooter getting to his full height.

Making an elementary mistake.

Presenting his entire body as a target.

Zeb taking his time.

Because he had the tiniest window for shooting.

Each shot had to count.

Even if the gunman returned fire.

Which he was trying to do.

The shooter was bringing his HK to his shoulder.

His movements smooth. Unhurried.

And then he was jerking.

Zeb's first round blew a hole in his shoulder.

The second bullet brought him to his knees.

His body falling.

Zeb flying away from him.

But taking one last shot.

A round that tore through the killer's head.

Zeb heard screaming and shouting from below.

'Get away,' he roared. 'Go home.'

He let go of the cable.

Fell on a bench as people scattered, still gripping the Sig tightly.

His left ankle twisting awkwardly.

A woman shrieked, 'Don't shoot me.'
'I won't,' he gasped, and struggled to his feet.
Urgency flooding through him.
Because he now knew where Namir was.

Chapter 85

Zeb didn't need to warn anyone about shooters in the building.

People were running scared, rushing out of the building. Any further warning from him would turn the rush into a stampede.

That would be worse. They'll head home in any case. Call the cops.

While I deal with Namir.

He limped out, some women screaming when they saw his gun and the blood on his clothing.

'I'm with the FBI,' he called out. But it was futile.

Namir will know something went wrong.

But he won't do anything yet. Not until he is sure.

After all, he is holding a trump card.

Sara.

It had come to Zeb when he was swinging on the cable.

The reason the terrorist wasn't at the church with the rest of his men was so blindingly obvious that he cursed himself for not having figured it out sooner.

He's at Ashland's home.

He needs an insurance policy until he escapes. He'll

probably go over the Canadian border.

He checked the cell he had grabbed off Tahir.

Still no signal.

That would buy him some time, since Namir would have realized he couldn't contact his men.

He reached his pickup on the street. Climbed into it swiftly. Reversed it and turned around.

Reached into his pocket and brought out another cell. The one he had borrowed from Ashland.

'Ma'am. Five down. No innocents,' he squinted, feeling dizziness wash over him, as Clare came on the line.

'I am getting reports, Zeb. Radio and cellphone traffic. Unconfirmed reports of gunmen in Erilyn's church.'

'I am confirming those reports, ma'am,' he stated grimly as a cruiser flashed past. He thought he caught a glimpse of Schwartz at the wheel.

'I was one of those shooters. The others, terrorists, are all out of action.'

No congratulatory messages from her. His boss was ice-cool, matter-of-fact, as if they were discussing the weather.

Which was why she headed The Agency.

'SWAT's ten minutes away. State cops, too.'

'No, ma'am. We have one more problem. Namir is loose. I am betting he's at Ashland's house.'

Silence, while she processed his information.

'You need to—'

'Yes, ma'am. I am heading there. Schwartz, ma'am. All he should do is contain the scene. Reduce the radio chatter. He should not act on his own.'

'I'll handle it.'

Zeb tossed the cell away. Drove past Farloe Street.

Looked at it from the corners of his eyes.

The same vehicles he had seen when he had arrived with the girl.

He knew, because he had memorized the makes and the plates.

But there was a new one. A black SUV. Underneath a tree. Facing away from Ashland's house.

Namir's getaway vehicle?

Only one way to find out.

He reversed in someone's driveway. Knocked over a pot. Offered a silent apology and headed back.

He cut his speed almost to idling as he nosed into the street.

No sign of any occupant in the vehicle.

Hiding somewhere?

He straightened the wheel. Pointed the truck at the black vehicle.

And jumped out.

Alert. Sig down his side.

Ran to the rear of the driverless truck. Ducked behind it and followed it as the vehicle rolled forward.

The truck rammed into the SUV.

Which rocked back and slid sideways several inches.

No gunman showed up.

Chapter 86

Several houses faced the street.

No doors opened. No faces appeared at the windows.

If Schwartz is smart he will have made calls. Warned townspeople to stay inside. Away from glass.

Ashland's house didn't have a direct view to the crash, however.

It was just beyond a bend.

Why would Namir have a getaway vehicle parked away from the house? Zeb thought about it for a moment as he surveyed the street, hands on hips. Like a concerned citizen, seeking out the driver of the crashed vehicles.

Because he doesn't want to call attention to Ashland's house.

Where they are all holed up.

Waiting for some news from their friends.

Probably getting the grandfather to make calls to find out what's happening.

He had one last check to make.

That the SUV was indeed a terrorist vehicle.

He prised open a door with difficulty.

No clues on the driver's seat or in the glove compartment.

He looked behind the front seats.

Heaved an inward sigh of relief when he saw the mags on the floor. Forty-round magazines for the MP7s.

He inspected one quickly. Full.

The idea came to him when he tossed it back.

He went back to the truck, its engine still running.

Reversed it.

It separated from the SUV with a screech.

He drove it past the smashed vehicle.

Toward Ashland's house.

Cut its speed, as before.

Clambered out quickly just before the house came into view.

Circled to the rear.

Clamped his left hand to the tailgate and pulled himself up.

Despite his injuries.

Zeb's idea was to take Namir by surprise. Even though he would be expecting an assault.

The truck picked up speed as it moved down the slight descent in the road.

It bumped when it came onto the lawn and moved across the uneven surface.

Zeb gritted his teeth against the agony.

This won't take long.

Either I will finish them. Or I will die.

In any case, I will buy time for SWAT to get here.

Sara's face came to his mind.

The sheer terror in it when she spoke of Namir.

I won't die before saving her.
Ashland's house had two floors.
They'll all be on the ground floor.

The front door opened into a hallway. Which led to a living room. At the rear was the kitchen and dining room.

But in between the two was a second living area. Access through the hallway.

Zeb expected the terrorist to base himself there, since the room was windowless.

He stopped thinking.

It was time to act.

Because the truck had crashed into Ashland's house.

Chapter 87

Zeb fell to the ground, using the vehicle's body for cover.

Sped to the side of the house.

A window ahead of him. The first living room.

He ran toward it and along the room's length, away from the front. Crouched beneath the window.

He started counting in his head as he imagined the scene inside.

Five.

Four terrorists. Two captives.

Namir shouting instructions.

Check out the crash. Watch out for police.

Four.

Two men would fan out.

One shooter would stay with Namir.

One would come to the living room.

Three.

The other would go to the rear.

Living Room man would come cautiously.

Two.

Body away from the window.

Trying to see through the glass. From all possible angles.
HK up.
Zeb rolled the stone he had picked up in his hand.
One.
Raised his hand.
Flung it against the window.
It shattered.
He imagined the shooter flinching.
On cue, a wild burst of fire shattered the quiet.
Splinters of glass flew.
Above him. Toward the front.
Giving him a rough idea where the shooter was.
Zero!
Zeb surged up.
The Sig chattered in a controlled arc, sweeping the room.
In the direction of the incoming fire.
Saw the killer, just as the killer spotted him.
Zeb corrected.
His rounds blazed in a left-right, up-down pattern.
Bringing the gunman down.
Something stung his cheek. A splinter of glass nicked his eyebrow.
Then he was inside the house.
Moving fast. Picking up the dying man's HK. Removing a handgun and putting it in his waist.
The hallway in front of him as he headed to the door.
House entrance to his left. Stairway to the upper floor to his left as well. More hallway and the second living area to his right.
Kitchen farther away.
'Nazar? Did you get him?' Two voices overlapping each other.

Both speaking in Arabic.

Sara screaming.

Ashland, strained. Trying to calm her.

Zeb knelt.

Snapped a quick glance at floor level, around the door.

Clear.

Got to his feet.

Entered the hallway cautiously.

A round crashed into his shoulder, bringing him down.

Chapter 88

Round came from behind. Shooter on stairs.

Zeb twisted even as he fell, flinging himself to the side.

His HK rising. Shredding the hallway apart. Paper and wood chips filling the air. Rounds whistling past his head.

His body jerking when one more round smashed into his chest.

His eyes unwavering, intent on the killer who was leaning over the bannister.

Zeb's shots nailing him, tossing him back, until the terrorist fell limply.

The girl screaming and crying. Namir shouting for his men to reply, not knowing how large the attacking force was.

Zeb got to his feet, sluggishly, automatically.

Turning his HK to cover the second living room's entrance.

No one else appeared.

Zeb knew he was in bad shape.

The round that went into his back had lodged somewhere high, near his shoulder.

The right side of his chest was bloody where the second slug had pierced.

His older wounds had opened.

He could move, however. He could hold a gun. He could fire. That was all that mattered.

He could see, even though his vision was fading at the edges.

'I have got the girl. And the old man,' Namir screamed from inside.

Zeb didn't reply.

He went to the first living room.

Leaned over the dead killer to haul the body up, biting his lips to stifle a groan.

He couldn't reveal he was badly hit.

Maneuvered the body into position.

Put his left hand around it, supporting the body's weight with all his strength. Keeping it as upright as possible.

His right hand holding the HK, providing additional support.

He shuffled slowly toward the terrorists.

'Who are you?' Namir called out.

Zeb thought he heard choppers in the distance.

His head was ringing, however. He was breathing loudly, harshly. Sucking as much oxygen as he could.

His animal brain readying his body for one last fight.

They will be near the far wall. Spread out. Namir with the girl, since she is the more valuable hostage. The other killer with Ashland.

He got closer.

Controlled his breathing.

Got his hands as low on the body as possible.

He knew they could hear him approaching.

It couldn't be helped.

He checked the floor.
No shadows to give away what he was attempting.
Took a quick mental check.
Good to go.
Well, not good, but there was no choice.
He flung the body inside the living area.

Chapter 89

Zeb threw himself to the floor and crawled forward swiftly.

A barrage of shots peppering the body.

A snapped look.

Namir in the left corner. Cowering behind Sara.

The other shooter in the right. Half-hiding behind Ashland.

All of them standing.

The terrorists realized their mistake—that they were firing at a dead man.

Whose body was falling.

Too late.

Zeb's HK was ripping.

Tearing into the wall behind the second terrorist. One slug catching him in the shoulder.

Ashland diving away, sensing that the killer was distracted.

Giving Zeb all the angle he needed.

He emptied the mag into the terrorist.

Who fell.

The firing stopped.

But Namir kept yelling.

Hiding behind the girl.

His eyes flicking between Ashland and Zeb.

'Don't move. I will kill her.'

Zeb tossed his HK away.

'Don't shoot,' he told the man in Arabic. 'I am getting up.'

He put his hands to the floor and heaved himself up.

Groaned loudly.

'You are the man in the forest,' Namir snarled.

'Yes.' Zeb studied him as he swayed on his feet.

The terrorist was unrecognizable from his pictures.

'Switzerland?'

'What? How do you know my language?'

'You got your face altered. Maybe in Switzerland. Or Brazil.'

'I got the girl. I will kill her,' Namir screamed, jamming the barrel of his HK against Sara's temple.

'You won't. Hear that sound? That's the FBI. You need a hostage. Her. You won't kill her.'

'I will kill her. And then kill you.'

'How will you escape, then?'

'You Americans,' Namir jabbed the girl, making her whimper. 'DON'T MOVE,' he yelled at Ashland, who was rising.

The grandfather got back to the floor, his face scrunched in fear.

'Don't kill her. Please. You can have me,' he whispered.

'I will kill you also,' Namir spat. 'Did I tell you how I killed your son? In front of his daughter?' He gouged the barrel in Sara's side.

'I was waiting a long time for that. FIVE YEARS.' He tried to kick Ashland, but couldn't reach him. 'I was in prison for that long. Because of your son. It all ends today.'

'It ends now.'

His fingers tightened.

'I am sorry, ma'am.' Zeb looked directly into Sara's eyes.

'Huh?' Namir blinked. 'What are you—'

Thought to action took a fraction of a second.

Zeb's right hand flashed to his back.

Grabbed the Sig tucked behind.

Brought it around and to the front.

Another fraction of a second.

While Namir was still trying to comprehend.

Zeb shot Sara in the shoulder.

She shrieked. Ashland shouted.

Sara sagged.

Her full body weight catching the terrorist by surprise.

Namir's upper body was exposed.

He let the girl fall. Turned his weapon around desperately.

Zeb's first shot punched through his forehead.

His second blew a hole through Namir's chest.

He felt himself hit somewhere in the chest.

But he kept on triggering. Two more rounds that threw the terrorist back.

And then Zeb was falling.

His Sig dropping to the floor.

He thought he heard something crash.

It didn't matter anymore.

He slipped into darkness.

Chapter 90

Epilogue

Zeb was still in Erilyn a week later.

In Pete Ashland's house.

The two rounds in his chest had come close to killing him.

One had missed his lung by a hair's breadth.

The other bullet was lodged deep.

He required eight hours of surgery, performed by a team of doctors Clare had arranged.

Sara's shoulder healed faster. Zeb's shot had been a clean one. It had not damaged bone, and the round hadn't pierced any vital organs.

Her operation had taken a couple of hours and, by the next day, she was up.

Ashland's living room had been turned into an operating theater for the injured.

The entire ground floor was like a hospital.

Clare had hard-looking men and women protecting the house.

She hadn't called back The Agency's operatives. Zeb's

friends still thought he was hiking in the wilderness.

It hadn't been difficult for Clare to hide Zeb's involvement. She had juice.

She had a brief call with the FBI director. Spoke to Idaho's governor and to the director of the state police. All parties agreed that SWAT and the cops would take credit for preventing a terrorist attack.

Schwartz praised all the law enforcement officers involved.

'That man in the church? Swinging on a cable?' he laughed at reporters. 'That was a SWAT officer. No, sir. He can't be named.'

The world's media flooded the small town and interviewed its residents. Not one person could identify the cable man. They went by Schwartz's statement.

Schwartz, the FBI director, and the director of the state police arranged several press conferences.

They announced that Namir, the world's most wanted terrorist, had been killed.

They acknowledged that no one knew how he and his men had entered the country.

They paid their respects to Kenton Ashland, whose body had been recovered. The dead campers' bodies had been brought back as well.

The president called Pete Ashland and expressed his condolences. He spoke briefly to Sara, who stuttered and stammered and ended the call teary-eyed.

A massive investigation was underway to backtrack the terrorists' movements.

Camera footage from airports was being studied. Namir's laptop and cellphone were being recovered, as were the weapons and the vehicles.

'You are lucky,' Clare told Zeb on the seventh day, when she had finished briefing him from a chair in the living room, next to his bed.

He was mobile, his upper body covered in dressings, as was his thigh.

From outside he could hear the bustle of Sara and her grandfather in the kitchen.

The house had been cleaned up. No trace of blood or any marks on walls remained.

The night of the shooting, a cleaning crew had arrived. They had answered no questions. They had gone about their business and, by the next day, the house smelled of disinfectant and fresh paint.

The bodies, the bullet holes, and the blood on the floor had vanished.

The Agency at work. Protecting not just its own, but also those who had helped.

'Yes, ma'am.' Zeb rose and flexed his arms.

He wasn't as good as new, but he would get there.

'Why don't you want the twins, the others, to know?'

'They haven't taken a vacation in a long while, ma'am. They would cut it short if they knew. Even though I am alive.'

Cool grey eyes studied him.

Her lips twitched in a small smile.

'They won't be happy if they find out.'

'I'm sure they won't,' he replied drily, imagining the outrage on Beth and Meghan's faces.

She laughed, then quickly became sober.

'The memorial service is tomorrow. Sara wanted to hold it when you were awake. And mobile.'

Erilyn had arranged a small ceremony in honor of Kenton

Ashland, the dead couple, and the hikers Namir had killed.

Sara had been adamant that Zeb stay back for it. She had brushed away his apology for shooting her, insisting he stay on for the event.

He had reluctantly agreed, after getting a promise from her that he wouldn't be mentioned or introduced to anyone.

'She needs—'

'She'll get all the help she needs. Counseling. Help with college. Anything. You saved her. And Pete Ashland. But she saved you, too.'

'Yes, ma'am.'

The grandfather had come to his bedside one night when the girl was asleep.

He had sat next to Zeb, a comfortable silence. Which he had finally broken.

'That day. When you came in firing. That terrorist—he could have shot me.'

'Yes, sir.'

Ashland regarded Zeb's expression keenly, his face showing no emotion.

'It was Sara that you wanted to save. Even if I died.'

'Yes, sir.'

'Even if you died.'

Zeb kept quiet.

Ashland's face crinkled and broke into a warm smile. Like the sun dispersing clouds.

'I knew it. I don't mind. Not one bit. Son, I have lived a long life. I would have died for her.'

He reached out and gripped Zeb's hand.

The event the next day was somber. The mayor made a short speech. Pete Ashland followed and spoke a few words. The crowd cheered and clapped when Sara came up to speak.

The choir came after, and filled the town and skies and the wilderness with singing.

Zeb left for New York that night.

He arrived at The Agency's Columbus Avenue office the next day and stopped in his tracks.

Beth and Meghan were at their desks.

Roger and Bwana were lounging on couches. Bear was inspecting a gun, along with Chloe.

Broker was practicing his golf shots on a small putting strip.

His crew were there.

Joy filled him, but he showed nothing of it on his face.

They greeted him. He concealed a wince when Bwana punched him on the shoulder.

He listened patiently when the sisters launched into their vacation stories.

'How was yours?' Meghan asked him curiously, when they had finished.

'The usual,' he replied.

'Hiking. Fishing.

'Some hunting.

'Some running.'

Coming Soon

The first in a new series

The Last Gunfighter of Space

The Cade Striker Series, Book 1

By

Ty Patterson

Bonus Chapter from
The Last Gunfighter of Space

The rider kneed his mount to a halt. Surveyed the town from a distance.

It was similar to hundreds of such burgs in the West.

A single boardwalk street. Dusty, twin tracks marking where carriages passed. The ground beaten down by the tread of horses and pedestrians.

Establishments on either side.

A bar. Wooden roof and front. Batwing doors. Doug's Drinking Hole. Black lettering on a white board, hanging on the front of the building.

A bank.

A general store. Fred's Emporium, a hand-painted sign proclaimed from its roof.

A hotel on the opposite side. Farther away, there seemed to be a blacksmith. More buildings that the rider couldn't make out from he where he was.

Hustler's Rock.

That was the town's name. Population of two hundred.

The rider stretched and looked around.

Ranches around town. Lush valleys. White dots that he

knew were cattle.

The town had been around for a while. It had started off as a trading post for settlers as they migrated West.

Then someone had discovered the river and the valley nearby. And almost overnight, the town's population had doubled. Then tripled.

First came the ranchers with their herds. The establishment grew around them. The bar followed. Then the general store, which doubled as the post office.

'What d'you say, hoss?' He removed his Stetson and wiped his hair down. 'Let's stop for a drink? My throat sure needs irrigation.'

His mount flicked its ears back in response. It didn't whinny or nicker. It knew the rider would do as he pleased. And it looked like, right then, a drink was high up on his list.

Not that the horse minded. It could do with some hay and water. They had traveled far. Mostly through desert.

At a click of the rider's teeth, the horse started forward again, puffs of dust arising as it walked.

The mustang was black with a white patch on its right shoulder and muscles that moved sleekly beneath its skin as horse and rider neared the town.

The rider guided it to the rail in front of the bar and dismounted.

He looped the reins lightly, taking his time, observing the town.

Mounted ranch hands drifted through, some of them dismounting beside him. A carriage rolled by, driven by a woman dressed in white. Her eyes cut to him, and she nodded lightly when he bobbed his head in greeting.

A man in a suit bustled out of the bank. A farmer loaded a

wagon outside the general store.

Hustler's Rock wasn't a peaceable town. It had a history of gunfights. Thirty men had died in one year.

There was no law. No sheriff. Ranchers ruled the town. What they said was law.

Just a drink, the rider promised himself.

Nevertheless, he hitched up his gunbelt, in which his Navy Colts were holstered and strapped to each thigh, and passed through the batwing doors.

The interior was cool, with a faint smell of sawdust in the air.

Four men playing poker in a corner table.

One man snoring at another.

A cowboy cleaning his gun. Sipping his drink.

Three men bellied up at the bar, chatting idly.

All patrons turned for a moment when the rider entered. Watched him briefly, then went back to their business.

The stranger spun a coin on the polished oak of the bar.

The bartender, a balding, burly man with sharp eyes, caught it deftly and brought out a bottle.

He eyed the rider as he filled a glass.

'Seen you somewhere.'

'Maybe,' the rider replied carelessly.

He drank deeply, savoring the fiery warmth that spread through him.

He closed his eyes for a moment, subliminally aware of the bartender speaking.

A hush had spread through the room when he opened them.

'You are Cade Stryker.'

Author's Message

Thank you for taking the time to read *RUN!* If you enjoyed it, please consider telling your friends and posting a short review.

Sign up to Ty Patterson's mailing list and get The Warrior, #1 in the USA Today Bestselling Warriors Series, free. Be the first to know about new releases and deals.

Check out Ty on Amazon, on iTunes, on Kobo, on Google Play, and on Barnes and Noble.

Books by Ty Patterson

Warriors Series Shorts
This is a series of novellas that link to the Warriors Series thrillers

Zulu Hour, Warriors Series Shorts, Book 1 (set before *The Warrior*)
The Watcher, Warriors Series Shorts, Book 2 (set between *The Warrior* and *The Warrior Code*)
The Shadow, Warriors Series Shorts, Book 3 (set before *The Warrior*)
The Man From Congo, Warriors Series Shorts, Book 4
Warriors Series Shorts, Boxset I, Books 1-4
The Texan, Warriors Series Shorts, Book 5
The Heavies, Warriors Series Shorts, Book 6
The Cab Driver, Warriors Series Shorts, Book 7

Gemini Series

Dividing Zero, Gemini Series, Book 1
Defending Cain, Gemini Series, Book 2
I Am Missing, Gemini Series, Book 3

Warriors Series

The Warrior, Warriors series, Book 1
The Reluctant Warrior, Warriors series, Book 2
The Warrior Code, Warriors series, Book 3
The Warrior's Debt, Warriors series, Book 4
Flay, Warriors series, Book 5
Behind You, Warriors series, Book 6
Hunting You, Warriors series, Book 7
Zero, Warriors series, Book 8
Death Club, Warriors series, Book 9
Trigger Break, Warriors series, Book 10
Scorched Earth, Warriors series, Book 11
RUN!, Warriors series, Book 12
Warriors series Boxset, Books 1-4
Warriors series Boxset II, Books 5-8
Warriors series Boxset III, Books 1-8

Sign up to Ty Patterson's mailing list, and get The Warrior, #1 in the USA Today Bestselling Warriors Series, free. Be the first to know about new releases and deals.

Check out Ty on Amazon, on iTunes, on Kobo, on Google Play, and on Barnes and Noble.

About the Author

Ty has lived on a couple of continents and has been a trench digger, loose tea vendor, leather goods salesman, marine lubricants salesman, diesel engine mechanic, and now an action thriller author.

Ty feels privileged that readers of crime suspense and action thrillers have loved his books. 'Intense,' 'Riveting,' and 'Gripping' are some of the descriptions that have been commonly used in reviews.

Ty lives with his wife and son, who humor his ridiculous belief that he's in charge.

Connect with Ty:
Twitter: @Pattersonty57
Facebook: AuthorTyPatterson
Website: www.typatterson.com
Mailing list: www.typatterson.com/subscribe

Made in the USA
Monee, IL
02 January 2025